THE OLD BROWN SUITCASE

OTHER BOOKS BY
LILLIAN BORAKS-NEMETZ

YA FICTION

The Sunflower Diary (Roussan, 1999)

The Lenski File (Roussan, 2000)

Slava (French translation of *The Old Brown Suitcase*
by Michelle Marineau, Les éditions Héritages, 1996)

POETRY

Garden of Steel (Ekstasis, 1998)

Ghost Children (Ronsdale, 2000)

ANTHOLOGY

Tapestry of Hope
(co-edited with Irene N. Watts, Tundra, 2003)

TRANSLATIONS
(UNDER THE NAME OF JAGNA BORAKS)

Dark Times: Poetry of Waclaw Ivaniuk
(Hounslow Press, 1979)

Astrologer in the Underground: Poems of Andrzej Busza
(with Michael Bullock, Ohio University Press, 1970)

The Old Brown Suitcase

A teenager's story of war and peace

LILLIAN BORAKS-NEMETZ

RONSDALE PRESS

THE OLD BROWN SUITCASE
Copyright © 2008 Lillian Boraks-Nemetz
First published 1994, Ben-Simon Publications

RONSDALE PRESS
3350 West 21st Avenue, Vancouver, B.C., Canada V6S 1G7
www.ronsdalepress.com

Typesetting: Julie Cochrane, in Minion 12 pt on 16
Cover Image & Design: Julie Cochrane
Paper: Ancient Forest Friendly "Silva" — 100% post-consumer waste,
    totally chlorine-free and acid-free

Ronsdale Press wishes to thank the Canada Council for the Arts, the Government of Canada through the Book Publishing Industry Development Program (BPIDP), and the Province of British Columbia through the British Columbia Arts Council for their support of its publishing program.

Library and Archives Canada Cataloguing in Publication

Boraks-Nemetz, Lillian, date
    The old brown suitcase / Lillian Boraks-Nemetz. — 2nd ed.

ISBN 978-1-55380-057-6

    I. Title.

PS8553.O732O4 2008   jC813'.54   C2008-900958-4

At Ronsdale Press we are committed to protecting the environment. To this end we are working with Markets Initiative (www.oldgrowthfree.com) and printers to phase out our use of paper produced from ancient forests. This book is one step towards that goal.

Printed in Canada by Marquis Printing, Quebec

In memory
of my father

ACKNOWLEDGEMENTS

I wish to thank Andrew Wilson
for his original editorial advice and
Dr. Robert Krell for his encouraging words.
I am also grateful to Ronald Hatch for
undertaking the revised second edition.

CONTENTS

Foreword

THIS BEAUTIFULLY written book by a child survivor of the Holocaust reveals glimpses of the horrors of loss, abandonment and fear no child should ever have experienced. It is a true account of the systematic deprivation to which Jewish children were subjected, with the final deprivation being that of life itself. Life in the Warsaw Ghetto was such that the author and others her age witnessed cold-blooded murders, the deaths of friends and family from tuberculosis and typhus, and desperation resulting in suicide.

By age ten, eleven or twelve, these children of the Ghetto had literally "seen it all." And yet, our author was lucky enough to survive as a chronicler, a witness to the events. Nearly one and one-half million Jewish children did not survive. They were not able to bear witness, to make a new beginning, to enjoy what life can offer.

The description of the re-emergence from a world of death to a world of life in Canada is one which should resonate in the being of every Canadian child of a refugee background. It is one thing to be an immigrant moving from one relatively secure place to another. It is quite different to escape a tragic past of torment and persecution and carry the enormous psychological burden of memories too terrible to remember but which nonetheless becomes a part of memory.

The author succeeds admirably in conveying the weight of the past while struggling towards a more hopeful future, all the while demonstrating clearly the complexities of transition.

How does one express oneself in a new language? How does one explain oneself? Will anyone understand? Will anyone care?

I too survived the Holocaust as a child. In the period of transition from Europe to Canada, I too was sustained by having several dear friends in childhood and adolescence. In *The Old Brown Suitcase*, the main character's friendships and her capacity to make friends and keep them offer a key to the puzzle of how to overcome adversity. A child needs a friend.

Perhaps this compelling story will influence its readers, young and old, to be more compassionate to newcomers, to those with uprooted lives — whether from overseas or from another school or neighbourhood.

Everyone suffer losses. No one lives life free of personal tragedies. A little kindness saved and salvaged a life which still enriches us today — fifty years after the destruction.

It reminds us of what might have been, had greater kindness and compassion existed in those dark days. Read and learn and remember.

— Robert Krell, MD
Professor of Psychiatry, University of British Columbia, & President, Vancouver Holocaust Centre Society for Education and Remembrance

CHAPTER 1

Far from Home

(MONTREAL, 1947)

MY LITTLE SISTER cried out in her sleep.

It was evening in Montreal, and darkness had descended upon the sweltering city. A white Cadillac carried my family and me towards an uncertain destination. The car was owned by Mr. and Mrs. Rosenberg, who had just met us at the train station and recognized our faces only through photographs sent them by my uncle from New York. We were to stay with them until we found our own apartment.

Mr. Rosenberg was pudgy, jolly and perspiring on this hot July night as he drove the big white car. Back at the train station, he had put his arm around me and said, "My you're a pretty little girl."

Hogwash. I knew I wasn't pretty, at least not at this moment, after the long trip. I felt like crying, that's what I really felt like doing. I wanted Father to hug me and tell me everything could be all right again. Instead, I smiled like a puppet.

My sister cried out again. Poor little Pyza was wide awake looking uncomfortable in the crowded car with only my mother's lap for a seat. Her face, chubby and round, was the reason we had named her Pyza — Polish for a dumpling. But now her blue eyes were all teary.

I sat wedged between Mrs. Rosenberg and my mother, who were trying to keep up a conversation in Polish. Their words travelled over my head and were drowned by my sister's cries. I felt that it was definitely up to me to pacify her.

"Shh, little one," I whispered and patted her fat little hand. Pyza looked at me with big sad eyes. Sometimes, when she looked at me that way, she reminded me of our other sister, Basia, who was lost somewhere in Poland.

"Once upon a time . . ." I began making up a story about three sisters who got lost in a storm but miraculously found each other again. Pyza stopped her sobbing, and before I had finished my story she was fast asleep.

Mother and Mrs. Rosenberg were still conversing over my head. I leaned back and looked at Mrs. Rosenberg, who sat tall, straight and thin in a grey dress. Mother's eyes were attentively focused on Mrs. Rosenberg's face, but there was a look of weariness in them.

"What is your older daughter's name?" asked Mrs. Rosenberg. She must have forgotten, because we'd been introduced at the station.

"Slava," answered Mother.

Mrs. Rosenberg delicately clasped her hands.

"Slava may be a lovely name in Poland, my dear Lucy," she said to Mother, "but it won't work here when she goes to school. Hasn't she another name, something more familiar to Canadians?"

"Elzbieta is her first name," offered Father, from the front seat.

"Elzbieta is better because it can be Elizabeth," said Mrs. Rosenberg.

Elizabeth? It felt like some other person. Just like "Irena" had felt when I saw it written in my false documents, back in Poland during the war.

"El-i-za-beth!" I repeated silently. With the pronunciation of "th," my tongue curled like a worm and my cheeks felt hot. What right did this lady have to dismiss my Polish name?

Father sat in front with Mr. Rosenberg. Their conversation sounded a lot more interesting.

"You know of course that Quebec is primarily a French province," Mr. Rosenberg was saying. "But the English minority has the upper hand. The French are treated as if they were a minority, and they resent it."

"And how do we Jews fit into all this?" asked Father.

"Have no fear," said Mr. Rosenberg with a smile. "Of course there is anti-Semitism. There is always that. But Jewish people are fairly safe here on most fronts, and we do well professionally. You're a lawyer, aren't you?"

"Yes, I had a good practice in Poland before the war." Father looked pensive. "Now I must find work. European law is much different from Canadian, so I will have to relearn everything in English."

Father's back was very straight and his head erect, while Mr. Rosenberg's balding head was round, set so deeply between his shoulders that you could barely see it. Although Mr. Rosenberg's hands were on the steering wheel, I had the curious feeling that it was really my father who was steering us towards our new destination. Just as he had always done.

I closed my eyes and wished that we were back in Warsaw, even in all its ruin.

The car stopped in front of a big house with a brightly lit porch. We gathered our things and climbed the steps. I sat down on my scuffed brown suitcase and waited.

The door opened and a young girl came out.

"*Dobry wieczor*," she greeted us in Polish with an English accent.

She was a bit taller than I, with brown hair and eyes. Her blue high-heel shoes matched her suit, and her hair was coiffed in perfect waves. She wore a bright red lipstick and matching nail polish. She must be a lot older, I thought.

"This is our daughter, Ina," said Mr. Rosenberg. Looking at me, he asked, "how old are you?"

"My name is Slava, and I am almost fourteen," I replied with emphasis on Slava. Once again my cheeks felt on fire.

"Our girls are the same age," said Mr. Rosenberg enthusiastically. "They must have a great deal in common. Come on, everyone, let's go in and get comfortable."

I pulled my suitcase into the hall and looked at Ina. She looked so sophisticated. Compared to her I didn't feel a day over ten, especially when I saw myself reflected in the large hallway mirror. Was that really me, that small girl with short, mousy-blond, and every-which-way curls, wearing a child's sailor dress and thick beige stockings with black oxfords, one tied with a piece of string because the shoelace had broken on the train? I looked hideous. If only they had let me keep my long braids. But they hadn't. It was all the fault of a lady on the boat that had taken us away from Europe. She had told my parents that my braids would look "positively outlandish" in America. So the next day they cut them off. I had saved the braids, still tied with red ribbons, and placed them in my old brown suitcase.

Mrs. Rosenberg said that we should all wash up before dinner.

"Come on, whatever your name is, we've got to get ready for dinner," said Ina in broken Polish. "I am in charge of you now."

How insulting, I thought. A voice inside me said, "Tell her again that your name is Slava." But I said nothing and followed her up the stairs.

"Come on. I'll show you to your room," said Ina yawning. We went up one more flight of stairs to a large bed-room with an alcove.

"This is your room," said Ina pointing to the alcove, and this is your door," she snickered, pulling the curtain across the alcove. With a final "see you at dinner," over her shoulder, she left me.

So this was my room, with a couch and a dresser. It had a large bay window and below it, a bench with coloured cushions. I sat on the bench and stared out the window at the shimmering city below.

It could be Warsaw risen from the ruins, I imagined, and this could be our apartment, and this window, the window of my own room. But this city was not Warsaw, and my room had been destroyed in the war, and this was the house of strangers.

"Hello, Slava, my little daydreamer." Father's voice was warm and familiar. His face appeared from behind the curtain. Although he was smiling, he looked tired. "It's time for dinner. I want you to be pleasant to the Rosenbergs. They are so very kind to let us stay with them for awhile."

I jumped up from the bench and hugged him.

"Tomorrow we will explore Montreal together. Would you like that?" Father asked, putting his arm around my shoulders.

I felt better and went slowly down the stairs to dinner. After all, Father was right. It was kind of the Rosenbergs to take us in when they did not even know us.

At dinner, I filled my plate with bread. The aroma of

bread, its freshness, made me more than just hungry. It had been six long years, always longing for that extra piece of bread when there was never enough. I remembered the long lineups in the snow waiting for a ration of one loaf of bread per week.

"Why are you taking so much bread?" asked Ina in a disgusted tone. "Don't you know that it will make you fat?" My mouth was too full to answer. Why did she have to act so superior?

The grownups drank toasts of vodka, and talked about Poland. From their conversation I gathered that the Rosenbergs came to Canada before the war. Early on, Mrs. Rosenberg waved her hand and said that she did not wish to discuss the war.

"It is too tragic a subject, particularly in front of the children," she said. I knew about the war; they didn't have to hide it from me.

I guessed that she meant to protect Ina, but why? I felt like escaping to the alcove but knew that this would displease my parents.

Mother and Mrs. Rosenberg started to talk about registering me in school as Elizabeth. That name! It sounded so harsh compared with Slava. Surely Mother would agree!

"Slava," Mother's voice interrupted, "isn't it time for bed?"

That was just what I wanted to do. Leave. I had not noticed until now, but Ina had already disappeared. I got up and said good night.

On the way upstairs I saw a light under what I guessed

was Ina's bedroom door but decided not to stop. Suddenly
her door opened. She must have heard my footsteps.

"You're not going to bed already?" she asked quizzically.
"Come on in for awhile."

I remembered Father's instructions to be nice to the family, so I agreed. Ina's radio was on. I didn't feel like talking
and would have preferred to listen to music. Ina went over
to her night table, picked something out of a bowl and
tossed it over to me.

"Here, have one of these," she said.

An orange! A whole one all to myself! I peeled it quickly,
and began to eat. The delicious juice dribbled down my
chin and throat, its scent filling my nostrils.

"Why do you eat so fast, so greedily?" asked Ina with a
sarcastic grin on her face. "It's only an orange."

I stopped eating and stared at her, humiliated by the way
she looked at me.

Because I haven't eaten oranges for six years, I answered
inwardly. Because there were no oranges in Poland during
the war and none afterwards when peace finally came. Because I was often close to starvation. But I said nothing. She
wouldn't understand.

I finished the orange in silence and excused myself, still
clutching the peels in my hand.

I paused in the hall for a moment to listen to the music,
then went upstairs. My parents' room was dimly lit by a
pink frilly lamp. I tip-toed past my sister's crib towards the
alcove, but stopped when I saw pictures of Mother and

myself on the bedside table. I walked over for a closer look.

On top of the small pile of documents lay an open passport. There was an eagle in the centre of a page, and below it, my mother's name and description. At the bottom of the page was printed, "Republique Polonaise" and "Rzeczpospolita Polska," both meaning the Republic of Poland. On the opposite page was a photo of Mother, along with a smaller one of me marked "Daughter." Beneath it was my description: Elzbieta Slava Lenska, born on September 5, 1933, in Warsaw, Poland. Eyes green. Hair blond. Female. At the bottom there was a round stamp: Canadian Customs and Immigration, Port of Entry — Halifax, July 1947.

I could hardly believe the picture was mine, taken only a few months ago with my braids still intact. It was the only picture left of me. The rest had been burned during the war, along with my birth certificate. I knew it had been done by my parents for my safety, but I resented it. Couldn't they have just hidden them? Could all traces of a childhood be so completely destroyed? Well, I thought, not completely. I would never forget Poland and my life there even though my parents wanted us to behave as if we were born the day we got off the boat. New people, new lives.

I went into the alcove, undressed and lay down on the couch-bed. But sleep would not come. Words and events milled inside my head like crowds in a park on a Sunday afternoon. Was I suddenly to become an Elizabeth? What about the Slava of the past fourteen years?

I jumped out of bed and went into the corner where my

suitcase stood. It seemed so long ago now that my father had given it to me, but its leathery smell and smoothness of skin remained the same. Despite the scuff marks from so much travel, it was as dear to me now as the day I received it. My fingers pressed its rusty catches and sprung them open. Right on top lay my two blond braids still tied at the bottom with red ribbons. The tops were held together by elastic bands. I laid them aside trying not to think of their history. When the ends were roots, I was only a baby.

Next, I took out pieces of a crumpled dance costume, and smoothed them out on the carpet. First, a hat with its golden petals of organdy and black velvet centre. Then a green satin bodice with more golden petals swelling out at the hips. I added the finishing touches by laying out the green satin leggings and green ballet slippers at the bottom, and placed my two braids on either side of the hat. There it was, my sunflower costume suddenly emerging like a phantom dancer.

I continued to rummage through the suitcase and came upon two tattered books: the Canadian novel *Anne of Green Gables*, and the Russian novel *Princess Dzavaha*, both in Polish editions.

At the bottom of the suitcase were several poems and stories I had written, and then some photos: one of Father before the war, another of dear Babushka, my grandmother, and finally a snapshot of my other little sister Basia, lost somewhere in an unmarked grave in Poland.

I thought of the destroyed pictures of my childhood and tried to rekindle them in my mind, like the candles that people light in memory of the departed. And I could see them before me rising out of flames.

CHAPTER 2

The Ballet

(WARSAW, 1938)

TODAY I AM FIVE years old.

It's my birthday, and Father is taking me out for a walk. Masha, my nanny, buttons my coat and hands me over to Father.

"Be good," she says.

Father and I walk hand in hand down our street, Aleje Jerozolimskie. It is a wide boulevard lined with trees still green in September. There are many cafes and shops where we stop to look in windows.

A small boy dressed in ragged clothes stretches out his hand and asks for money.

"Children shouldn't handle money. Wait here," says Father to the boy. We walk into a delicatessen and Father buys bread, some oranges and chocolate. He hands the parcel to me.

"Here, you give it to him."

The boy's dirty hand takes the parcel; his big eyes brighten and he runs off pressing the food to his chest, as if he had just won the biggest prize of his life. I take Father's hand and hold it tight.

In the evening after a lovely birthday and many gifts, I kiss Mother and Father good night, and go off to my room with Masha. It is time for bed.

"Don't forget to say a prayer for all those who love you, your mother and your father," says Masha. "Especially your mother," she adds mysteriously.

Lately, Mother's stomach has been getting bigger and bigger. One day she disappears without an explanation, and I do not see her for several days. I ask the cook and the maid if they know what had happened to Mother. But all they do is look at each other and sing silly songs.

Finally I ask Father.

"Tomorrow I will take you to her," he promises. I can hardly wait for the big secret to be revealed.

The next day Father and I walk into a grey stone building. There are people in white everywhere, as well as people in ordinary clothes. Father explains that we are in a hospital, a place for the sick. Is Mother sick? I wonder. We go up the elevator and down a spotless corridor into a white room. Mother is lying in bed. She does not look sick. She is smiling. There is a little bed next to her big one.

"This is Basia, your new baby sister," says Mother.

A baby lies in the crib, all wrapped up in a blanket.

Finally Mother comes home with my new baby sister. Everyone tells me that a stork brought her.

In the mornings I sneak around the crib to observe the minute red face, toy-like hands, curly hair and round cheeks. She is much prettier now.

I want to go to Mother and ask her if she still loves me, but I can't find her. The baby keeps her busy, so I spend a lot of time with Babushka, my father's mother. She lives on Marshalkowska street. She is my favourite grandmother, and I love her very much.

Now that I am five, Babushka has decided that I am big enough to learn how to read and write. Every day at four o'clock in the afternoon, we sit at the big dining room table, and I learn how to read and write the alphabet. It is a whole new world.

Ballet school is another new world, and in it I am learning to speak French. I feel silly each time I have to curtsy to the head mistress, Madame Fleuri. But my parents tell me that this is how well-behaved young girls should act. Only French is spoken here. "*Bonjour, Madame,*" and "*Au revoir, Madame,*" I say, trying to roll the r's to the back of my throat.

One day I come home with exciting news. Madame Fleuri

has chosen me to dance a solo in the ballet's annual gala at the Grand Theatre of Warsaw. I will dance the "Oberek," a Polish national dance. It is very fast and I love it. You have to dance many different steps and pivot and hop from one foot to the other. Madame Fleuri has explained the theme. It will be a garden where butterflies, birds, flowers and other garden things will dance to celebrate life. So I must get a costume made, and it will be in the style of my favourite flower. That doesn't take any time to decide. I love sunflowers best.

Mother and I take a *dorozhka* on our way to the dressmaker. It's a carriage driven by a horse. We can watch the streets and the people, and the clopping of the horse's hooves along the pavement sounds like a musical instrument. The driver wears a navy-blue dash cap. He has red cheeks and a long whip. I love the *dorozhka*.

We are bringing packages of materials for my costume. We ride for a long time across the city and finally through a part of Warsaw that is not as pretty as my own Aleje Jerozolimskie. Finally we arrive. Mother gives the driver a few coins and tells him to wait.

We enter a building and go through a corridor into the courtyard, then down the stairs into an apartment. A woman greets us, smiling and bowing to Mother. Her apartment is dark and shabby. Mother hands the woman our parcels and the woman opens them.

Out come clouds of green satin and golden tulle, and suddenly the room is no longer dark or shabby.

"We need a ballet dress with a green bodice, a skirt of gold petals, a gold-petalled hat and green satin leggings," instructs Mother. The dressmaker makes a sketch. How can she make all that? I wonder excitedly. On the way out, the dressmaker assures us that the dress will be ready within a week. And she keeps her word.

On the day of the dress rehearsal I put on my costume. It's like a cloud, a burst of golden petals on a green stem. All my classmates clap in praise, and even Madame Fleuri comments, "*Très, très jolie, Mademoiselle Lenska.*"

On the evening of the performance, I am so excited I cannot think of anything else. Father drops me off backstage and kisses me for good luck.

My classmates are magically transformed. There is Ola the swan, Felix the bird, Joanna the butterfly and many more flowers. There is even a big red strawberry, a blueberry and a raspberry. The stage is set with green trees and grass. With only half an hour left before the performance, I can feel goose bumps all over.

Madame Fleuri, dressed in black, her grey hair tied up in a knot on top of her head, lines us up. We enter the stage in order of performance, and sit down on the grassy floor, forming a background for the dancers.

The orchestra below the stage is making musical sounds, but the great curtain is still closed. Then all is still. Madame Fleuri reminds me that I go on first.

The orchestra starts playing, and the curtain slowly opens

to loud clapping from the darkened theatre. I get up, but my feet feel like stones. The stage lights are blinding. I run up to centre stage and pause. Should I dance in this garden for the other flowers and creatures, or should I dance for the dark mass that I can barely see? My decision is swift. The music of the Oberek begins. I dance, and forget all about the performance, my fear and blinding lights. I fly with the music as it swells the air. I can barely stop with the music, and I make my bow, just as we rehearsed it.

There is a strange hush in the theatre. None of my classmates are clapping. Do they not like my dancing?

Madame Fleuri comes up the stage and asks me to dance again, this time facing the audience. I am embarrassed. What have I done? I turn around and all of a sudden there is thunderous clapping and laughter coming from the dark pit below. I want to run off the stage but my feet won't move. Yet I must dance again, I must. The Oberek theme begins once more, but this time my dancing feels different. I am more aware of my steps, and of the darkness in front of me. Afterwards, I bow again, this time towards the audience. Everyone stands up and claps.

The rest of the show seems a dream. I watch my classmates perform and wish for the very beginning so that I could undo my mistake.

Backstage, Madame Fleuri says, "*Très bien fait, ma petite.*" Father and Mother come to take me home. "You were wonderful," they say. No one mentions my mistake. Other par-

ents come for their children. They look at me and smile.
Perhaps my mistake was not so bad after all. Father picks
me up and carries me to a waiting taxi.

At home in my room I cannot sleep. My body vibrates
with the music of the dance. Through the crack in the door
I see light from Father's study across the hall. I tip-toe to his
door and peek in. Father is rehearsing a speech for court. He
walks back and forth speaking out loud, his hands behind
his back. I turn around to go back to bed and see a square
object standing next to the wall. A shiny new suitcase; in the
faint light I can see that it is brown. I bend to lift it; I can
just handle it, I think. But it falls to the floor with a thump.

The study door opens and Father walks into the hall.

"Aha, you found it, my little snoop," he laughs. "Why not?
It's yours!" He puts a key into the lock and the suitcase
opens. There is an envelope inside.

"Open it, since you can read now," says Father.

I tear the envelope open, and find two train tickets to
Michalin, where Grandfather has his villa. My beloved villa
with its garden full of sunflowers and sweet berries.

"Next weekend you and I are going on a trip, my little
one," says Father. "I bought this suitcase so that you can
pack your things in it. You're getting to be a big girl, Slava.
Who knows where this suitcase might take you someday.
Do you like it?"

Do I like it! I put my arms around my father's neck. Not
at all like a big girl.

CHAPTER 3

The Sirens

(MONTREAL, 1947)

THE NEXT MORNING, Ina avoided talking to me at breakfast. She quickly excused herself saying that she had to run or she would be late for tennis.

"I don't suppose you play tennis," she said to me as she rushed out the door. There was no time to reply.

"Slava has had to learn to survive for the past six years," said Father to Mr. and Mrs. Rosenberg. Did I hear a slight bit of annoyance in his voice echoing my own unspoken feeling? Father continued, "She has not even been to school yet, let alone learned how to play tennis."

The Rosenbergs looked at each other.

"Perhaps she should have an English tutor before school starts?" suggested Mrs. Rosenberg. This time my parents looked at each other, and I knew why. We could not afford it right now. All we had was a monthly check from my uncle in New York. It was just enough to cover our basic needs. Mother thanked Mrs. Rosenberg for her concern about my English, but said that this was not a good time for a tutor, since we might only be in Montreal a few weeks.

"Come on, Slava, let's get ready for our walk," called Father. For the moment I could forget learning English.

The quiet street was lined with trees. It was in an area called Westmount, Father explained, where wealthy English people lived. We walked past large brick houses like the Rosenbergs' that were set into spacious gardens.

It seemed strange to see houses instead of apartment buildings on the city streets. In Warsaw people lived in apartments, and houses were to be found only in the countryside. On Aleje Jerozolimskie, there were many shops and cafes. Warsaw's streets were always busy with people coming and going. But here in Westmount there were few people walking on the street.

We turned onto a street called Sherbrooke. It looked more like a proper city street with its larger buildings, dress shops and streetcars. There were more people too.

I heard two languages spoken. I guessed that one of them was English. The other sounded similar to the French I had learned in Warsaw but not quite the same. Still, just knowing that there was French spoken here made me feel closer to home.

Soon we came to another busy street called Peel Street. It was fun reading the different street names: some in French, others in English.

The streets were getting busier and Father announced that we were finally "downtown." We had been walking a long time, and decided to stop for lunch.

"There is a restaurant somewhere on Peel street called Child's," said Father consulting his map. "It was highly recommended by the Rosenbergs."

We found Child's along Peel street just off St. Catharine. It was a strange looking restaurant, compared to the elegant cafes of Warsaw. The narrow tables had high-backed benches on either side. You had to slide into them, and ended up sitting next to a wall. A waitress came and asked us something in English. Father ordered using a new word taught him by Mr. Rosenberg: "pancakes."

The waitress brought two plates, each filled with a stack of five flat round cakes. There was melted butter floating on top. Then she put a glass container filled with thick, dark liquid on the table We looked at it not knowing what it was for.

"Maple syrup," said the waitress, pointing at the dark liquid container. "You put it on top of the pancakes like so," she said tilting the container and pouring the liquid over my cakes. Father thanked her. She was kind, I thought, and must have understood that we were foreigners.

They were oozingly delicious, these "pancakes," covered with the sweet, golden "maple syrup." We also drank a dark sweet fizzy liquid, called Coca-Cola.

After lunch, we continued our walk in downtown Montreal, passing movie theatres, shops, restaurants and churches. Stopping at a street corner, I looked up and saw a mountain in the distance. On top stood an enormous cross, like a beacon in the bright July sun.

It was getting hot and crowded in the streets. Father was wiping his forehead with a hanky, and my clothes were sticking to my body, but we continued our walk. Soon we came to an older part of the city, with cobblestone streets. The buildings looked similar to the ones in Warsaw before the war. They were narrow and very close together, built of grey stone and red brick with slatted wooden windows, high doors with arched entrances and black iron gates.

Further down the street there was a throng of people in front of an old building. As we approached, we could smell smoke. Flames were shooting from the roof of the building and people were standing at the windows, screaming and gesticulating. I grasped Father's hand and held it as tight as I could.

Then, above the noise of the crowd I heard a shrill and whining noise. A siren coming closer and closer.

"Papa, it's an air raid," I screamed tugging at his hand. I wanted to drag him away, but we could not move because we were wedged in between masses of fascinated onlookers. A long red truck pulled up across the street, and men in steel helmets began to unravel a long hose. Soon it squirted water at the furious flames, while more sirens sounded.

My head was exploding with visions of burning buildings and thunderous crashes. I caught a glimpse of a man who was laughing. Why was he laughing? I let go of Father's hand.

"Slava," he shouted, "this is Canada! There are no bombs here. It is only a fire, the war is over!" But all I could hear were sirens wailing in my ears.

I ran past blurred faces and windows, tripping over the holes in the pavement, seeing only dark cellars and faces of frightened children.

CHAPTER 4

The Soldiers

(WARSAW, 1939)

I AM SIX.

I hear airplanes in the distance, and I am running towards a building for cover. I pass a baby in a carriage under a tree. I stop to look at her. She is wearing a pink bonnet, and her blue eyes look up at the sky. I can't see Father. Where is he?

An airplane roars above; people are running. The baby starts crying. I don't know what to do. I try to stop several people to tell them about the baby, but they just rush past me.

Suddenly masses of planes thunder over the city. Father appears out of nowhere, running. He picks me up and carries me into the building and down the stairs to a cellar. Although there is whistling and crashing above us, it feels safer inside this dingy place, even though it smells of dampness and mould. The temporary shelter is crowded with people, some sitting on wooden benches, others on the floor. All look terrified. The men have their arms around the women and children. A woman is weeping; a child wails.

Someone says that when you hear a long whistle, a bomb is about to fall on a building. We hear a whistle now, and I plug my ears and close my eyes. The whistle goes on and on. Will the bomb hit our building? There is a deafening crash, but when I open my eyes we are still here. The bomb must have fallen somewhere else.

As suddenly as it began, the grinding roar of the bombers subsides. All is still. No one moves.

A woman rushes into the shelter, carrying a bloody bundle with a pink bonnet. She is young and pretty in a polka-dot dress, but her eyes are filled with tears.

"My baby is dead," she cries crumpling to the floor.

We stare dumbly at her and at each other, while she wails on the dusty floor. I listen to her sorrow, still seeing the baby's innocent blue eyes looking up at the sky.

Father walks over to the woman and gently tries to help her up. Several women follow. One takes the bundle out of her arms. Another puts her arms around the woman's hunched shoulders and leads her out of the shelter.

We walk out of the darkness of the cellar into daylight. It

is the same warm autumn day outside, only now it's darker with the particles of grey dust and smoke from the burning buildings. The carriage under the tree is smashed; pieces of fallen brick and steel lie all around us.

I am frightened. What has happened to the rest of our family?

We rush home to find that both Mother and Basia are safe. But my mother's pale face scares me. She looks ill.

"I was just having tea when the bombers came. We ran downstairs," she says. "Everyone was gathering in the courtyard, and when some people ran down to the cellar we followed. It was horrid, just like the raid this morning. Basia cried the whole time."

"I am sorry that we weren't home. I was very worried about you," replies Father, hugging her.

The German army is getting closer to Warsaw. Masha stays, but our cook and maid leave for their homes in the villages. We are sad to see them go.

The radio calls for all Poles, young and able, to join the Polish army to fight the Germans who have invaded Poland. Father says that he must join up even though he doesn't want to leave his family. He promises to return soon. The day he leaves, Mother takes a thin gold bracelet off her wrist and gives it to him for good luck.

When Father kisses us goodbye, both he and mother have tears in their eyes. I look at them through a mist of tears blurring my eyes. We watch Father disappear down the corridor.

Mother tells me to pack my brown suitcase with my most important things and some clothes as well, because we may have to leave at any time. I take two of my favourite books and my sunflower costume. Mother helps me pack and shakes her head, unable to understand why I need the costume.

The days pass and there is no word from Father. I am not allowed to go outside. After standing in line for hours, Mother brings home rationed bread and potatoes.

The air raids continue to devastate the city. We seem to be constantly running to the shelters as the sirens sound. There is no water or electricity. We burn candles and carefully ration cans of preserves we keep in the pantry. We drink the syrup from the jars of fruit preserves, which we dilute with the water that Masha brings in a pail from the Vistula River.

Everything seems to be in a state of terrible confusion. The windows are closed and the drapes drawn most of the time. It is so hot I can hardly breathe. Often in the middle of the night I wake up from nightmares, screaming.

The booming sounds of guns are heard all the time in the distance. Mother says that half the city is in ruins. One evening we are sitting around the dining-room table when someone knocks on the door. Masha goes to the door and opens it.

A bearded man with dirty, tattered clothes stands on the threshold.

"Stefan!" Mother cries, and rushes up to him.

It's Father. He looks worn and chalk-white. He tells us he

has walked for miles, and has been without food for the last three days. Mother ushers him into another room. I want to go with them but Masha stops me. I wait impatiently for what seems a long time, then the door opens and the "old Father," clean-shaven and elegant, comes in. I run to him and hug him.

Over tea and bread, Father tells us the story.

"We didn't have a chance. The German Army is a powerful war machine, and there was no way we could hold them back for very long. I was wounded in the leg on the second day. Our regiment ran out of ammunition and there were masses of casualties. The Poles fought bravely, but it was an impossible fight to win. Our army pulled back and fell apart. We were told to disperse and fend for ourselves." He sips his tea and continues.

"The roads were full of trucks and retreating infantry. I made my way through the fields and forests trying to avoid the road. My leg hurt and bled, so I tried to stop at farmhouses to get help, but the peasants were suspicious and frightened and didn't want to help me. One day I saw an old peasant riding in a cart full of hay drawn by a tired nag. With the last bit of strength I had left, I hopped on the cart from the back and hid in the hay and rode part of the way to Warsaw. The old man didn't even know I was there. He was drinking vodka all the way."

We look at Father's leg. Mother has bandaged it with a clean dressing, but already there is some blood on it.

"Don't any of you worry, I'll be fine," says Father. "I am just so happy to be back."

Mother puts me to bed, and I have no bad dreams. Father is back at last.

A few days later, we hear marching feet, the screech of vehicles, and loud voices from the street. We rush up to the window: the street is crowded with German soldiers and tanks.

"Get away from the window," says Father. I look at him not understanding.

"Jewish people are going to have to be very careful from now on," he says. "Hitler and his followers are out to get us."

I don't understand why the Germans don't like us. And who is Hitler? I want to ask. But my parents look so upset that the questions freeze in my throat.

Several weeks later, we come home after visiting friends, and find our apartment in ruins. All the glassware and china lies shattered on the floor. The floor of my room is littered with pages out of torn books and stuffing taken out of my animals. Most of the furniture is gone.

Father says that the Gestapo, the German police, must have traced our apartment as belonging to Jews. They are destroying Jewish shops in Warsaw, and evicting Jewish families from their homes.

My parents decide to restore the apartment the best they can and continue to live there, despite the threat of possible eviction. There is no other place to go. Also, since there is a housing shortage in Warsaw, my room is rented out. I sleep with Masha now and miss my own room. But soon Masha leaves for the country, and I have her room all to myself. She leaves me a long string of beads with a cross, and tells me to pray regularly.

Winter passes and then the spring. One day in late summer, Father and I venture out for a walk.

German soldiers in green uniforms are everywhere. They speak loudly in a language I don't understand; they always seem to be marching rather than walking. Some have helmets and rifles. Others wear caps and carry pistols in black leather holsters. They have high, very shiny black leather boots. The worst wear black uniforms and caps with the skull and cross-bones on them. They look sullen and angry.

Father doesn't seem afraid, but he avoids main streets and we walk down the smaller narrow ones.

Through a space between two buildings I see men building a brick wall.

"What are they doing, Papa?" I ask.

"They are making a Ghetto," Father replies. "The wall will close off a portion of the city and all the Jewish people of Warsaw will be forced to live there."

A bearded man in a black coat passes by. He wears a white arm band with a blue star on it. He is not the first person I have seen wearing the star. After the man has gone by, I ask Father about it.

"These arm bands have been forced on the Jews. The star

is the Star of David. Your mother and I already have ours, but we don't always wear them. If you don't, and you are caught, you are badly punished," he explains.

"Will I have to wear one?"

"No, children under twelve don't have to wear them." Father sounds tired and irritable.

I still don't know what a Star of David really is, so I ask.

"David was the king of the Jewish people a long time ago . . ." Father doesn't finish.

A motorcade of Germans is passing by. Father takes my arm and quickly steers me into another side street. His step quickens, and I run to keep up.

Later at home, I think more about the blue star. The Star of David. I like the sound of it. Anyway, it looks much better than the swastikas, those twisted crosses the German SS wear on their uniforms. They are black and ugly.

In the months to come, the wall grows higher. Father says that in some places it is already eight feet high, topped with barbed wire and jagged pieces of glass, to prevent people from climbing over to escape.

CHAPTER 5

Sunlight

(MONTREAL AND STE. ADÈLE, QUEBEC, 1947)

"*LA PETITE PAUVRE*," said an old man. People bent over me, exclaiming in French as I sprawled hot and breathless on the steps of a church. Father had finally caught up with me. He picked me up and took me to a nearby coffee shop. While I sipped a cold drink, he tried to assure me that the war was in the past, that there was peace now in the world, and I mustn't be frightened by the memory. But my memory of war lingered on the way home. I felt dazed. The past and the present had melted together.

The next day, Mother took me to a Polish doctor recommended by Mrs. Rosenberg. The doctor felt my stomach, listened to my heart and lungs, took a blood sample from my finger, and told my mother that I was anaemic. He recommended vitamins and liver.

That evening I sat down to a plateful of liver and onions. Ina grimaced at the sight of it. "It's like a blob of mud topped by browned weeds," she said.

I couldn't eat it and my parents didn't force me to. Instead, they gave me some tablets which felt like cement stuck in my throat.

I forgot all about the tablets when dessert came, a banana split prepared by Mr. Rosenberg.

"Try *that*, young lady," he said, bowing, as he placed it in front of me. I had never seen anything like it: a glass dish full of vanilla ice cream, topped with whipped cream, chocolate sauce, cherries and cut-up bananas. The mixture was unbearably delicious, and I couldn't stop eating. Before long, Ina and I had our faces messy with ice cream. It seemed to me that Ina ate her banana split just as greedily as I had eaten my orange the night before.

Soon after this, my parents decided to leave Montreal. Lodgings in the city were too expensive, and we couldn't stay on at the Rosenbergs' indefinitely. The Rosenbergs suggested a moderately priced *pension* in the village of Ste. Adèle and offered to drive us there.

I was glad to leave. Ina didn't want to come with us, so we said a polite but stiff goodbye in Montreal.

Soon we had left the city's hot grey pavement and thick

air for the gold and green fields of the Quebec countryside. Peaceful villages emerged, surrounded by wooded hills and farms.

As we went further into the Laurentians, we passed lakes that looked so clear and cool I wished we could have stopped and jumped into their bluish-green water. Finally I saw a sign that read Ste. Adèle, and after another kilometre the car stopped in front of a large farm house.

It was nothing like the *pensions* my parents and I had visited at Polish summer resorts. There, the resort buildings were large, elegant and white. Usually they were set inside orchards or surrounded by rose bushes and trees, and were close to the water and forest. In contrast, this Canadian *pension* was a sprawling rust-coloured wooden farm house with a wrap-around veranda. A tawny cat sat in one of the windows while chickens cackled on the side of the yard behind a wire fence. Two trees graced the front yard, and several flower beds brightened the entrance. No one was in sight to greet us. We took our luggage from the car and went in, walking through a wood-panelled hallway into a lounge. Mrs. Rosenberg surveyed the room with a look of distaste that said it wasn't anything like her elegant home in Westmount. I liked it a lot.

Two large couches and three brown velvet chairs stood welcomingly on a worn, rose-coloured rug. The couches were covered in beige fabric with a faded pattern of red roses. The velvet of the chairs was quite bald in places. Here and there stood wooden tables with china animals and ash-trays; several floor lamps with frilly shades bowed over the couches and the chairs. Above the mantle of a red brick fireplace hung a painting of a farmer loading his wooden cart with wheat, his horse standing patiently as several children looked on. Surrounding the farmer and the children were fields and wild flowers.

The room smelled of mildew, mothballs and lemon, which brought back the memory of Babushka's cottage in the Polish countryside.

The Rosenbergs wanted to leave, so we followed them out onto the veranda. Mrs. Rosenberg and Mother exchanged goodbyes with the usual niceties.

"You must come and stay with us again soon, my dear Lucy," said Mrs. Rosenberg sweetly, to which Mother replied with equal sweetness. But I had the impression that Mother didn't really want to stay there again. Of course she couldn't say that, could she?

Father and Mr. Rosenberg shook hands heartily, and Mr. Rosenberg offered his help if we needed anything. Somehow I felt that he really meant it. We watched from the porch as they drove away in a cloud of dust, leaving us suddenly alone and apart from the rest of the world. At least with the Rosenbergs, we could communicate in our own language.

A small, slim woman came out of the house onto the veranda. Her blond hair was done up in tight curls, and she wore a dress patterned like the couches in the lounge. Her

face was oval with a straight nose and wide blue eyes. She
was attractive in an angelic sort of way. When she shook her
head the curls bobbed up and down like springs. I couldn't
tell her age. I was fascinated by her red furry bedroom slippers.

"Please enter," she beckoned. "I speak no much English
only *français. Je m'appelle Marie.*"

Father spoke to her in French, only twice having to look
up a word in his French/Polish dictionary. As she described
the rules of the house and the meal times, I found I could
understand her. It was wonderful to know that we could
communicate with her, even if it meant sometimes using a
dictionary.

Marie showed us upstairs to our rooms. In the room
where my parents and Pyza were going to stay, everything
was green from the wallpaper to the scatter rugs and bedspread. I followed Marie's furry slippers up a steep wooden
staircase to an attic.

It was hot and stuffy, but when she opened the window
the country air dispersed the heat. The room had blue corn-
flower wallpaper, a wood-panelled sloping roof, a blue-
patterned bedspread and a desk and chair under the window. Above the bed hung a cross, and next to it a picture
of the Madonna in a sky-blue robe, her hands gracefully
folded and her face demure and peaceful. I had seen such
pictures in Poland in the homes of Catholic country folk.
Most of all, my eyes were drawn back to the window. There,

below the azure sky lay an emerald field, and beyond it swelled the hills, covered with dense forests.

Between the field and the forest stood a white church, its steeple gleaming gold in the sun. I stood enchanted, remembering the farm in *Anne of Green Gables*, which I had read in a Polish translation. Marie tried to tell me something in English but I didn't understand. I said, "No speak English," amazed that I knew enough to say anything. But when she pointed at the bedpan under my bed, I nodded in recognition. Of course I had seen one of these before. Then she pointed to a wash basin and white enamelled jug standing on the desk. She explained in French that when I wanted to wash up, I could bring some water from the bathroom downstairs. I said *merci* and she smiled and said that she must go downstairs and get the dining room ready.

Soon after Marie had left, Father came upstairs and announced that it was dinner time. I told him how well Marie and I had communicated, but I didn't mention my first attempt at English, which still felt like sticky rubber in my mouth. The dining room had two long tables for the guests, who lived either in the farmhouse or in the nearby cottages. A girl about my age came up and said something in English, but I couldn't answer, so she shrugged her shoulders and went away.

"See, you're going to have to try and learn English soon," said Father watching us. Of course he was right.

Dinner was meat pie, vegetables and potatoes, followed

by ice cream with chocolate sauce. I was hungry and ate very quickly. I was glad that Ina wasn't there to watch me.

After dinner I wished that the girl would come over again. I tried to catch her eye, but she didn't seem interested.

Marie was busy clearing the tables. Her cheeks were flushed and her hair fell in limp wisps about her face. She looked over and smiled, and I wanted to go up to her, but instead I just sat there tied to my chair. If only I were as brave as that girl who came up to me before supper. So free and unafraid. All of a sudden Marie motioned me over to where she stood. Had she guessed my thoughts? She looked as if she could use a helper. I went over and offered myself. At first she hesitated. When I insisted, she gave me a tray and pointed to the dirty glasses on the table.

In no time the dining room was cleared and set for breakfast, and Marie invited me into the kitchen for milk and cookies. Before I knew it, I was learning French phrases and grammar.

"*C'est pour cela que je t'ai fait venir*," said Marie. "Teach you *français*," she added with a warm smile and closed the grammar book. Then she suggested that we go upstairs as it was getting to be bedtime.

She took up a jug of water and waited as I washed up and prepared for bed. Just as I was about to climb into bed, she raised her finger, as if to say, not yet, and she lifted her eyes to the cross above the bed. She knelt next to the bed and motioned me to do the same. Then she crossed herself, and looked at me as if I should be doing likewise. I did it only so as not to offend her.

Then she lowered her head and said, "*Prions.*"

I began the Lord's Prayer in Polish just as Masha had taught me when I was little, without my parents knowing. Marie looked at me with surprise.

"What language?" she asked.

"Polish, *polonaise*," I said in both languages.

"Oh . . . *polonaise*," she exclaimed. "*Je suis canadienne-française, et vous êtes canadienne-polonaise.*"

"*Pas encore canadienne*," I replied.

"*Pas encore canadienne, mais vous êtes catholique, n'est-ce pas?*"

I felt numb and couldn't answer.

"*Bon*," she said patting me on the back. She smiled at me warmly as she left the room.

"I am Jewish," I said quietly. But the door had already closed behind Marie. Why hadn't I told her right away? I asked myself in the darkening attic. Anne of Green Gables would not have held back the truth. You're a coward, I told myself.

The moon had flooded my room with an eerie light, its pale glow illuminating the face of the Madonna above my head . . .

I woke up in the morning to the sounds of chickens cackling, cows mooing and birdsong. The room was filled with the smell of earth, a pungent blend of grass and manure.

Outside the attic window, sunlight bathed the corn field. The forest beyond the field stood dark and silent. I will explore the forest, I promised myself, and ran downstairs for breakfast. Marie, in a blue dress, hair tied back, served juice to the vacationers. She smiled in greeting when she saw me and said, "*Viens cet après-midi. Je t'enseignerai un peu de français.*" A French lesson in the afternoon? I nodded in agreement.

My parents were already seated at the table.

I told Father about the picture of the Madonna in my room and asked him what it meant to the Christians. He looked somewhat surprised and said, "In the Christian religion it is believed that Mary, the Virgin, had her son Jesus by immaculate conception. This means she didn't do what wives and husbands do together in order to have a child. She bore a child whose name was Jesus. Christians believe he is the son of God. But the Jewish people believe only in the one Almighty God." Father finished and looked at me inquisitively.

I didn't really understand what he meant, and wanted to ask him more, but just then Pyza started to cry and my parents busied themselves with her.

I slipped out quietly into the garden and wove my way through the corn to the adjoining field. It was full of poppies and dandelions, but nowhere could I find my beloved sunflowers. I walked across to the forest.

This shady forest with its soft green moss and ferns could

as well have been the forest in the village of Zalesie, where I lived with Babushka during the war.

How strange that happiness and sunlight could disappear from one day to the next, or one place to the next. Yet sunshine and darkness can exist side by side, I decided, seeing my own shadow outlined against the grass, black, like that sunny day in Poland when the light in my life had suddenly dimmed.

CHAPTER 6

The Ghetto

(WARSAW, 1940)

I AM SEVEN.

It is a sunny November day, but I am cold.

An endless dark line of us moves slowly through a gate in the tall brick wall. People carry on their backs or push in carts all that remains of their life's belongings. They enter the Ghetto beneath the cold eyes of German soldiers and Polish police. A cruel silence reigns over us despite the voices, the shuffling of feet, the grinding of wooden carts against the cobblestone street and the clanking of pots and pans. The faces of the people around us are frightened. Some are crying as they walk.

I walk with my parents, my hand numb from the weight of the brown suitcase. It contains all I have: one chipped porcelain doll, two books, my ballet costume and some clothes. My father carries two large cases and a knapsack, while Mother holds my sister. Basia is only two years old.

We step through the gate away from sunlight, into the grey shadow of the Ghetto.

All of a sudden Mother stops as if she can't walk any further. A red-faced soldier yells "*Schnell! Schnell!*" into Mother's face, telling her to go faster, and hits her on the back with a thick black baton. Mother stoops beneath the blow, her face twisted with pain, and moves on, with Father next to her, his face sickly white. Basia begins to wail. The soldiers are shooting at some people huddling in the door-way of a building. As we pass by one of the soldiers points his pistol at us. There are gunshots all around. Behind me I hear footsteps of the soldier's boots, and another shot. My knees crumple and I sink to the ground. Am I dead? No, the bullet was for an old woman who fell to the ground behind us. Father pulls me up and whispers, "Quickly, these mad-men will kill anyone who disobeys them." I look back. The old lady lies where she fell, and people step over her body.

As we stumble further away from the gate, the immediate feeling of terror only slightly wanes.

"I know how terrifying all this is," says Father, "but we must be brave, Slava." He is breathing hard under the weight of the luggage, and his face is still white. "You're not going to give up now, are you?"

"No, I am not giving up, Papa," I answer, still shuddering, my lips stiff and unwilling.

My mother walks in silence, staring ahead. Basia is quiet.

Finally we arrive at our new home. The walls of the building are greyish and shabby. The stone facade is chipped and yellow in places and the windows are dirty. We enter through the courtyard, and find the inside even worse. Masses of people mill up and down the stairs and in the corridor of our apartment, pushing mattresses and suitcases.

Through the doors that bang open and shut, I see sheets being hung around the beds, the only way to create some privacy, as in a hospital. Wrinkled sheets hang on crooked rods or string, swaying in the breeze of human motion. The three bedrooms, dining room and living room of each apartment are occupied by five families, twenty-five people who must share the one kitchen and bathroom. And the stench throughout the place! It smells of old plumbing and sweat, of garbage lying in corners, of dirt left behind by the previous occupants.

Our room is one of the large bedrooms of a common apartment, or maybe it's the parlour. Who knows? It is like the others, filled with the same stench and shabby furniture. Black, torn shades hang against the windows like crows that have frozen in flight. On the table stands a naphtha lamp, our only source of light for the long winter nights to come. A red velvet chair huddles in one corner, its crevices filled with dirt and dust.

I sit exhausted in the red chair and watch my parents make the best of what we have. They energetically clean, wipe and arrange our provisions on a shelf and put our clothes into a wardrobe. Meanwhile, they give me the job of entertaining my baby sister, who is marvellously oblivious to our misfortune. I try to make funny faces, and then, quietly, tell her the story of Little Red Riding Hood and the Big Bad Wolf. She listens attentively then begins to chortle. Her laughter is the only bright moment of this unhappy day.

Mother makes tea and puts out bread for supper. The tea is hot and sweet. The coarse bread is black and stale, but we eat it thankfully as if it were the best tasting meal on earth.

Someone knocks on the door. It opens and an elderly woman enters our room. She is chubby and poorly dressed save for a beautiful hand-knitted shawl around her shoulders and arms. Her heavy beige stockings are held in place by elastics just below the knee, and they bag at the ankles.

"I am Mrs. Solomon," the woman says hoarsely. "I would like to invite you to the Sabbath dinner tomorrow evening. We will share what little we have. Anything you bring will be welcome."

Suddenly she begins to cough. At first the cough is normal, but gradually it becomes so violent that my parents rush to her side. They sit her down with difficulty as her large body heaves with spasms. Pulling a handkerchief from a soiled sleeve of her dress, she presses it against her lips. I offer her my cup of tea. She takes several sips, and when the cough subsides somewhat, she continues.

"These are terrible times for Jewish people. Before this awful thing happened we lived in a big apartment on Marshalkowska Street. The Germans took everything from us, even the samovar my mother brought all the way from Petersburg in Russia. They killed my husband on the street because he refused to undress in public." She wipes tears from her eyes. "Now my daughter Sallye and I share one room with my brother and his wife and her sister. All in one room! They say that over a hundred thousand people entered the Ghetto today, and that there will be more to come. Where will they live?" she cries. "Where is the God of our people?"

Mrs. Solomon grows silent and her body rocks back and forth as if in prayer. No one speaks, it is getting dark. Father lights the naphtha lamp and pulls down the blackout shades. Mother offers Mrs. Solomon a cup of tea but she declines.

"Thank you, but I must go. Sallye, my daughter, has not been well lately. The doctor thinks it could be tuberculosis. But please come to our dinner tomorrow night." She smiles, and for a moment her tired face brightens, as if some inner light had turned on. "We must continue to live in spite of all this, at least until tomorrow," she says, and leaves.

"What is tuberculosis, Father?" I ask.

"It is a disease of the lungs," he replies, shaking his head sadly. "A very contagious disease. Her coughing makes me wonder if poor Mrs. Solomon doesn't have it too."

"Papa," I say, "I noticed blood on her handkerchief after she coughed. She tried to hide it."

My parents look at each other sadly but say nothing. I go to bed. The light of the naphtha lamp casts eerie shadows on the walls.

I sleep fitfully, half-dreaming about poor Mrs. Solomon and her daughter Sallye. Do I hear coughing across the hall? I want to say a prayer to God and include them. But I am uncertain after today. I wonder if Mrs. Solomon is right. Could it be that God no longer hears our prayers?

The morning brings with it a jumble of sounds. There are feet shuffling past our door, voices behind the walls, cries, wailing, angry shouts, women's, men's and children's voices.

"There is a long lineup to the bathroom," announces my mother after looking out into the corridor. "What are we going to do?"

Father dresses and goes out for half an hour and returns with a bedpan and a pail. We all feel better in a while. He takes the pail out, while Mother washes out the bedpan with water taken from the kitchen, which she pours out later into the toilet.

Every Friday night my parents, Basia and I go to Mrs. Solomon's for a Shabbat dinner. The eight of us just fit around Mrs. Solomon's long brown table. I sit between my parents and Sallye.

Mrs. Solomon wears a black lace scarf on her head and lights the Shabbat candles. Her hand circles over the flames and she says a prayer in Hebrew, a language I don't understand. Afterwards, she looks up towards the ceiling as if it were heaven, her eyes full of tears. I like the sound of this language and the solemnity of the prayer. Her daughter translates it into Polish for those of us who don't understand Hebrew. It is a prayer to God that gives thanks for the food and asks for His blessing and deliverance from our present condition. At the end of the prayer everyone says "Amen." Mrs. Solomon weeps.

We are now given bowls of watery soup with dark bits swimming in it. Then potatoes are served with something that resembles chicken. It is boiled, with mostly yellow skin hanging from the meagre bones. It tastes slimy. There are pickles and jam on the table. Mrs Solomon tells us it is practically the last of her own preserves that she brought to the Ghetto.

"Does the Lord hear our prayers?" I ask Sallye after the meal.

"Of course He does," she answers cheerfully.

"I like the idea of Shabbat," I confide to Sallye. "We never had it in our home, only sometimes at our friend's house, but I can barely remember it."

At night I say my own prayer to God.

I like Sallye very much. She treats me like an adult, and plays with me when she feels well. She sings Yiddish songs, some of which sound sad, some happy. She says that it doesn't much matter whether you understand the words, the Jewish soul comes through the sound. On this and other Friday nights we listen to Sallye after dinner and then clap, asking for more songs. Our lives become less dreary on Shabbat nights.

Sallye is becoming terribly skinny, her skin transparent like yellow tissue. She coughs more frequently now that winter is upon us, and sometimes stays in bed all week. I want her to get better, but one morning I awake to the news that Sallye has died during the night. I go back to bed and weep into my pillow. I vow never to pray again.

Mrs. Solomon is hysterical for days. Shortly after Sallye's death, she becomes very ill. As days go by, I avoid looking at the soiled and smelly pile of sheets outside her room. One day they carry her body out on a stretcher. Our Shabbat dinners resume after a while in someone else's room, but they do not feel the same.

A sign appears in the courtyard and on the outside of our building:

QUARANTINED — TYPHUS

The gate to the courtyard remains open, because our whole street has been quarantined. But the food grows scarce because no one is allowed in or out beyond a certain point. Are we going to die? I wonder about it each night as I lie in bed. Often I hear a young boy cry out in pain from an apartment above us. I listen, helpless. In the mornings he sits in the window, white as a ghost. His mother tells everyone that he has a nervous stomach.

One night I hear nothing. Maybe he is better. But in the morning they carry him away. He died of typhus, and he was only fourteen.

A few days later I am playing hide-and-seek in the courtyard with the other children, when I am nailed to my spot by a scream. I look up. The mother of the boy who died stands in a window on the second floor. Her hair is wild about her face and she screams and screams. Suddenly she lunges forward and falls out of the window. She is falling towards me, but I can't move. Her body lands next to me with a thud.

Choking on tears, I run out of the courtyard into the street. But soon I am forced to stop, for the street ends abruptly at the high wall of the Ghetto, a quarter of a block from our building. I stand panting in front of the wall. This part of it is made of wood. Down below there is a space between the wood and the cobblestones, and through it I can see the soldiers' black polished boots, marching back and forth, back and forth. I hear men laugh and speak in their harsh-sounding language, which I have come to fear and hate. I turn around and walk back very slowly to the courtyard.

Life goes on.

Mother combs my hair thoroughly everyday, because it is through lice that typhus spreads, and lice love to get into hair. She uses a special comb with two sets of teeth. Through luck and cleanliness, we escape the plague, and soon the quarantine is lifted.

One evening my parents tell me that I will be finally going to school, but that it must be kept a secret. Schools in the Ghetto are forbidden. No one must know in case the Germans find out.

In the morning, Father takes me to a building not far from ours but on another street. We walk down to a room in the basement where he leaves me, saying that he will be back at noon to pick me up.

The teachers are two young sisters. Fela is short, and Hala is tall. But both are skinny, have dark hair and wear glasses.

There are about ten of us children, both boys and girls. The youngest is six and the oldest is ten. We sit in two groups of five at separate round tables. The tables are very low, and the seats are wooden boxes with lids on them. Each table has a stack of exercise books, paper and pencils.

When introductions are over, Fela calls us to attention.

"Children, we are happy to have you with us," she begins, "but before we start our lessons I want you to listen carefully to the following instructions. Each of you is sitting on a bench that opens at the top. Inside it you will keep your books and drawings. If there is a knock on the door, I want you to put your pencils, books and drawings quickly into the bench. My sister Hala will be responsible for all the other things that have to be put away, while I will take care of whoever is at the door." We sit quietly listening to our teacher's words.

"If anyone asks what you are doing, answer politely that you are playing games with paper, glue, crayons and cards. Above all, do not mention the word 'school' outside of this classroom to anyone. No one must know what we do here. Learning is forbidden in the Ghetto. Breaking these rules can cost us our lives. Do you understand?"

We all answer "yes" in unison, with very serious faces. But soon we begin to enjoy ourselves. Fela and Hala are very patient. They laugh with us, and teach us songs and poems.

I can hardly wait from one day to the next to go to school. I am finally learning. There are stories to read and listen to, wonderful stories about life in Poland, geography and history, and even a bit of math. We draw and paint and make things out of coloured tissue paper. When the materials run out, we laugh, and puzzle over how to do a project for which there are no tools. When there isn't any coloured paper we use whatever paper we can find. When we run out of ink, we use pencils. Fela calls it "using ingenuity and common sense."

One day someone knocks on the door. Fela gives us our cue. We pick up our drawings, exercise books and pencils and throw them into our boxes. Meanwhile, Hala swiftly picks up the textbooks and disappears into another room. All that is left on the table are some playing cards. Fela goes to the door. But there is nothing to panic about. Just an elderly man looking for someone. He looks in and shakes his head.

"You are fooling with danger," he says, "but I admire your courage. I hope that you are also learning what it means to be a Jew."

Our teachers laugh. "We don't need to study being Jewish, we are living it!" says Fela. The man shrugs his shoulders and leaves.

I try to avoid our cold apartment and the courtyard with its screaming kids, stench of potato peel soup and laundry. I love only the school, where I feel a part of an important and secret society.

One day we sit in school as usual, while Fela outlines our work for next week. Books and papers are strewn all over the tables. Suddenly there is a loud knock on the door.

The children's frightened eyes are fixed on the teachers. My hands shake as we go through our drill, and I drop things. "Hurry, children hurry," whispers Fela.

She opens the door, and two tall men in black uniforms stride into the room. Their boots pound at the floor and the black swastikas stand out against their red arm bands. The shorter of the two bellows out at Fela in heavily accented Polish.

"What is all this, *Fraulein*? What are you and these children doing here?"

"We are just playing, sir. Children get bored doing nothing. We sing, play cards," answers Fela quietly.

The SS officers look around suspiciously. "You know that school is not allowed, *verboten*," he shouts at Fela, shaking his finger at her. "And you, who are you?" he asks, this time pointing his finger at Hala.

"She is my sister," explains Fela.

"Sister, huh?" barks the SS man and pokes Fela's shoulder with his finger. His companion snatches our cards off the table and puts them in his pocket. Without another word, but with hatred on their faces, the two officers leave the room. Their boots thunder up the stairs. Then all is still.

We sit silent as stones, reminded once again that we are helpless in the face of the enemy, and that learning is a crime.

Fela and Hala congratulate us on how quickly we carried out our drill, and as we leave the school they smile and say, "Don't worry, we'll see you all tomorrow."

But nothing consoles me as I walk home with a sick feeling in my stomach. When Father and I return the next day, the door is boarded up. On it is a placard that says in ugly black letters, "*Schule Verboten*," and other words I don't understand.

No one in the neighbourhood knows what happened to Fela and Hala.

Father tries to cheer me up. On the way home from school we stop at a building. "This is the orphanage run by Dr. Korczak, who is not only a doctor but also a writer of children's books and a great teacher," he says. "I want you to see the children. I have helped him on occasion to find food and clothing for them."

A woman greets us at the front entrance and says that she is Dr. Korczak's assistant. The doctor isn't feeling well today, but we can see the children. Many of the orphans are gathered in the main room. Their heads are shaved because of lice, and their bodies are almost skeleton-thin. These are the children whose parents are either dead or missing. But they smile at us and play and talk among themselves.

Once on the street again, I look up at the building and see an elderly man with glasses and a white beard watering flowers on the balcony. They are the only flowers among the twisted iron balconies and dark windows of the buildings on the street.

"That's Dr. Korczak," says Father. "He is a great man."

As we walk away, I keep turning around until the last red dot of Dr. Korczak's flowers disappears.

CHAPTER 7

Escape

(WARSAW, 1942)

I AM NINE.

In the months to come I resume playing games with the kids in the courtyard, but soon even that comes to an end.

The latest orders from the Germans are that everyone who wants to survive must work. Father already works for the *Werkschutz*, in the work shop Security Force. He arranges for Mother to work at one of the *Wehrmacht* work shops set up in the Ghetto by the German army, to fix uniforms and sew other things that the soldiers need.

Mother and I walk each morning to the Schultz Company. The room upstairs where Mother works is very long, filled with tables, sewing machines and workers.

Children are not supposed to be here, but Father makes special arrangements for me to get in, as long as I make myself as inconspicuous as possible.

All day Mother sews fur collars for German uniforms. I hide on the floor under the table and try to help by picking up pieces of fur and thread, but it feels stuffy and uncomfortable under the table. For lunch, the workers are given soup and sometimes a piece of bread. The soup looks like brown water and is tasteless, and the bread is stale. But it is all we have to eat for the entire ten-hour day. I am always hungry these days, so I feel lucky to have even that. The hunger makes us weak, and often I see Mother swaying on her feet from exhaustion.

When we walk to and from work, we see terrible things in the Ghetto. Children beg in the street. Dirt and garbage piles up, and huge rats scuttle in dark corners. We see a man shot because he refuses to bow to a German officer. We see another man hung naked on a tree by soldiers, who laugh at his nakedness. Old people are shot to death simply because German soldiers consider them useless.

The Ghetto is overcrowded. More than four hundred thousand people are living in a space where only a hundred and sixty thousand used to live. But now the German authorities want to send us away — those who have not died from sickness or starvation. The soldiers begin to raid different parts of the Ghetto and take people away. No one knows when their street or home will be raided next. Just in case, we keep our suitcases packed and ready. My own brown suitcase is beginning to look a little battered.

One early morning, they come to our building. We can hear their boots march into the courtyard. They shout in German, banging on doors. We wait in our room until they come, their black polished boots echoing up the long corridor. They come closer and closer, and then stop. A heavy fist pounds on our door. It bursts open and a red-faced soldier rushes into our room. He levels his rifle at us.

"*Juden raus!*" he hollers, telling us to get out, and his rifle follows us as we take our suitcases.

We file out of the building and join the others in the courtyard. Everyone lines up with their belongings at a table set up in the centre of the courtyard. As the officers check everyone's identity cards, they tell the people to line up in two rows. When our turn comes, the officer ignores the fact that my parents work for the German Shop and orders us to line up at the left. My parents say nothing. The soldiers herd us out onto the street where there is already a long column of people waiting. Jews, young, old and middle-aged. All look shabby, sick and starved. We line up with them and wait.

People whisper. Some are sitting on their bundles.

"Where are we going?" they ask one another. "What will happen to us?"

A man in a torn coat asks Father, "Do you know about the labour camps? They say that it's better there. If you work, you survive."

"There are so many rumours," answers Father. "People are taken to a collection place called *Umschlagplatz*, and then deported by train to some resettlement camp in the east. I am sure that is where we are going. But I don't know exactly what happens when we get there."

The soldiers order us to start walking. They stride alongside pointing their rifles at the moving throng. Although it is early fall, the day is cold and rainy. My coat and shoes are soon soaked through.

"Faster," shouts the soldier who ordered us from our room. His red face scowls out from under his steel helmet. He shoves an old couple forward with the butt of his rifle, and they fall to the ground. They lie there, while the soldier orders us to walk over them.

Another soldier beats a woman with a black truncheon. She falls screaming to the ground. The soldier forces her to get up and continue without her belongings.

I stumble. The soldier screams at me and hits me on the shoulder. I fall. Father instantly picks me up and steadies me. "Be brave," he whispers.

I don't feel brave. My knees are bloody, and my shoulder hurts, but I still hang on to the brown suitcase. I feel like an animal who is being punished for something. But what did I do? They drive us along in a pony-like trot. We cower beneath the menacing batons and guns, shoulders hunched over.

There are people lying on the sidewalks. Some dead, some

still half alive. Blood stains the pavement. Starved children with swollen bellies and bony legs hover next to the buildings, watching us pass.

Suddenly the column comes to a halt as shots boom out. I am lost in a maze of filthy coats and rags. Blue Stars of David flicker before my eyes. People push against me. Its hard to keep my balance. Then I find myself next to Mother, who is carrying my crying sister. I clutch Mother's arm with my free hand. When I finally let go, there are red marks in her flesh, where I have dug my nails. Father appears at my side and pulls Mother and me out of the lineup. "Run, run, quickly, through that gate!" He thrusts us forward. We run through an arched gateway into a quiet courtyard. No one follows us. Father leads us through an open door into a deserted apartment. We huddle in its dark corridor for what seems a long time.

Finally, Father breaks the silence, wiping the perspiration off his forehead. "It was a chance we had to take. We were only five minutes away from *Umschlagplatz* and the trains. I have seen them pack those cattle cars. They put so many people in each, how can they breathe? And who knows where they go from there. I've heard that they separate parents from children, and that no one comes back." Father's voice is weary. Basia is asleep, and Mother sits on the floor against a wall, with her eyes closed. We haven't eaten all day.

When all appears quiet, we leave and learn that we must find another place to live because our part of the ghetto has been liquidated.

Several weeks later Father hears a rumour that all the children in the Ghetto will be taken from their parents and sent away. No one knows where.

Father and Mother decide that my sister and I must leave the Ghetto. There are many questions I want to ask, but the troubled look on my parents' faces keeps me silent.

Each night I lie awake, terrible thoughts flooding my mind. Each day I wait for Father to tell me that I must leave. There is hardly any food, even at the factory. Except for the walk to Schultz I never go outside any more and it's almost spring.

I awake one morning with a fever.

My head hurts, my body is on fire. Through a mist I hear voices saying, "It's measles. She can't go anywhere." I toss and turn and sweat for days. Once when I wake up I see Mother standing over the cot. She is holding Basia, who is dressed in a coat and hat.

"Say goodbye to your sister. She is going away," says Mother quietly. Through a daze I try to focus on the bundle in a brown wool coat and a white hat with bunny ears. Two big blue eyes in a little face look down at me. What does she want from me? Can't she see I'm sick? I push her away, and turn towards the wall.

In the morning I wake up feeling better. The fever seems to have gone. The sun is shining outside. Where is everyone? I look around the room and see that Basia's bed is gone. I run to the wardrobe and see an empty shelf where her things once were. My God, I didn't know she was leaving for good.

I didn't even say goodbye.

That evening my parents make sure that my brown suitcase is properly packed. Although it is so full that it is hard to close, I refuse to part with my books and my sunflower costume. I beg and they let me keep them.

"Now don't be frightened," says Father almost cheerfully. "You will have to leave soon, but I don't know when."

I go to sleep feeling comforted but wake with a start.

Someone is shaking me.

"Hurry, hurry," says Father. Mother dresses me quickly and hugs me. As she says goodbye her voice is thick with held-back tears.

A minute later, Father and I are shivering on a misty street. It is dawn.

The street is deserted.

We walk quickly. I ask no questions, for I know what we are doing. When we hear the rumble of a truck approaching, Father pulls me into a doorway. An army truck passes, and we continue walking.

We stop at a half-burnt building. Father pushes at the front door, which squeaks open, and we walk into a dark apartment. It is empty, and Father tells me to sit on my suitcase and wait.

"Don't be scared," he says. "I am waiting for someone." He paces up and down as if rehearsing some speech in his mind.

The door squeaks again, and I jump. A man walks in wearing the cap and badge of the Jewish Police Force of the

Ghetto. Father greets him with a handshake, then takes a small jewellery box, a pair of leather gloves and a bar of soap out of his pockets and hands them over. The man opens the jewellery box, and in the dawn light something sparkles. It's Mother's diamond ring. The man stuffs the things into his coat pocket and leaves.

Father tells me to be patient. He tells me what I already know, that I am leaving the Ghetto.

I sit on my suitcase and keep silent. A rat scurries across the floor. Then another. I move my suitcase away from the squeaking rats, and Father stops pacing. He shoos away the rats and sits down next to me on the floor.

"If all goes well, you are going to your grandmother in the country," he says slowly.

Babushka! I will see Babushka! For a moment I am overcome with excitement. I feel brighter in this gloomy room.

"Are you coming too, Papa?" I ask.

"No, darling girl, I am not. We would be too conspicuous, and I can't leave your mother alone. Just remember what I told you. We can't let the Germans win. We must survive. So when the time comes, you must follow my instructions perfectly."

"I will, Papa," I mumble into his shoulder. My throat is choked up, but my eyes feel dry. I try not to cry.

As daylight approaches, I hear sounds I haven't heard for months. I hear streetcars and other vehicles, sounds of a normal city.

"Where are we, Papa?" I ask.

"Near the Ghetto gate to the other side," he replies, confirming my guess.

The policeman returns.

"It's all fixed," he says. "I gave them the goodies. They promised to pretend not to see her. But you know them; they can turn on you anytime. It's a chance you have to take. Good luck!" He salutes and leaves.

Father sits down on the floor again, this time with his head in his hands. After a long moment, he gets up.

"We're leaving now. Remember what I told you," he says, taking my hand and my suitcase.

We leave the building and walk for several blocks. We stop and Father squeezes my hand tightly.

About half a block from us is a busy checkpoint in the Ghetto wall. Three soldiers in steel helmets hold rifles as if ready to shoot. They march back and forth in front of the large opening. Several Polish policemen in navy blue uniforms stand by the opening.

"This is the way out of the Ghetto, Slava. You are going to cross the line in a few minutes," Father says gravely. "In the pocket of your coat is a false identity card. The name on it is 'Irena Kominska.' It says that you are a Catholic orphan from Warsaw. There will be a woman waiting for you on the other side. She will know you, and she will take you to Babushka's."

I am frozen. I say nothing. Father gives me the suitcase. My hand can barely hold it.

"When I tell you, start walking," he says. "Walk through the checkpoint at a normal pace. Do not hesitate, or run. Above all, do not turn around to look at me." He hugs me with tears in his eyes.

"Now go!"

I look at him for one last moment, let go of his hand, and begin the longest walk of my life.

I try to feel brave as I march towards the checkpoint. As I draw closer, the green German uniforms grow bigger, and the brass buttons of the Polish police coats gleam in the sunlight. I arrive at the checkpoint and begin to walk through. The gendarmes and the police do not appear to notice me. As I walk straight ahead, they turn away. My knees feel weak, and my heartbeat fills my throat, but I keep on walking. A few more steps and I am on the other side.

I hear shouting beside me.

"I know who you are, you little Jewess! I saw you!" A small boy in rags points his finger at me. I clutch my suitcase tightly as if it were Father's hand, expecting the worst. All of a sudden the shouting ceases as a tall woman in a grey suit grabs my hand and pulls me into a side street.

She stops for a moment to take my suitcase from me. "You can call me Agnes," she says. "Don't be afraid." Only then do I remember that Father had said someone would be waiting for me on the other side.

We walk quickly now. The beggar boy is left behind, but I feel that the whole world is staring at us. We rush into a train station. Agnes shows the conductor our tickets and we climb into one of the cars. It is almost empty. A few minutes later the train pulls out of the station.

Agnes sits next to me. She is wearing a grey hat to match her suit. Her eyes are grey too, but large and bright. She is fair-haired. I wonder if she is Jewish. But then, I am fair-haired too.

It is my first train ride in two years. I sit on the wooden bench, taking in things I haven't seen for so long. We pass by open fields and forests, peasants on carts filled with straw, cows grazing in the pastures, and farm houses with white curtains in the windows. The Ghetto wall is behind me. But I wish my parents and my sister were here. God knows when I will see them again.

As sleepiness overcomes me, I rest my head against the shoulder of the woman in a grey suit. It seems only an instant later that I hear someone say, "Wake up, Slava, we are almost there."

The voice is unfamiliar. Whose is it? Where am I? I open my eyes and see Agnes. Oh yes, I remember now. We are on the train going to Babushka. Agnes takes something out of her bag and hands it to me. A piece of bread and sausage. I almost swallow the food without chewing. It's so good.

The sun shines brightly as the train moves through the peaceful countryside.

"You've slept for an hour and a half. We should be arriving soon," says Agnes. She tidies my hair and straightens my dress. "You want to look pretty for your grandmother," she says.

The train slows down and passes a white sign that says ZALESIE, then stops. Agnes takes my suitcase and we get off. The station is deserted. We walk to a wooden hut set back from the tracks, almost hidden by trees. Agnes slowly opens a door that squeaks.

It's a general store. An old woman sits half asleep in a rocking chair, a floral shawl around her shoulders and a kerchief on her head. She sees us and gets up with difficulty.

"What do you want?" she asks in rural Polish, eyeing us suspiciously. Her mouth is toothless and her voice harsh.

"Could you please direct us to Spokojna Street?" says Agnes.

"Who are you seeing there?" asks the woman.

"A friend," replies Agnes.

The old woman stares us up and down, then gives us instructions, pointing her bony finger out the window.

We come to a road with small wooden houses on either side. As we pass by, curtains are pulled aside and faces look out at us. Yet there is no one to be seen on the road. No little kids play outside the houses. Only the occasional dog barks as we pass.

I am not afraid. I compare this peaceful village with the Ghetto, and I happily breathe in the fresh country air. Then I think of my parents and my happiness ebbs.

We turn into Spokojna Street and stop at a white house

with a white wood fence around it.

A curtain is swept to one side, and a face looks out for a moment. Then the door of the house opens and Babushka runs out. "Slava," she says, smiling and pecking me on the cheek. "My dear little Slava." Then she raises a finger to her lips and draws us inside. There, in the privacy of drawn curtains, Babushka hugs me tearfully and sighs.

"The neighbours mustn't suspect anything," she says. "I told them that I had promised to take in a friend's daughter."

Agnes stays for tea and gives Babushka my papers.

A man comes in. He is bald, heftily built, with a red face, and he is wearing black round-rimmed glasses. He is Babushka's husband, whom I have never met. His name is Vlad. He smiles in greeting and takes his tea.

Agnes says that she must leave.

"You are a very brave lady," says Babushka. "How will we ever thank you for bringing Slava to us?" She gives Agnes a jar of preserved pears for the road. The tall woman thanks her and kisses me goodbye.

"I hope to see you after the war is over," she says to me. "You are a brave little girl."

After Agnes is gone, Babushka takes my hand and leads me to my room. She beckons me to sit beside her on the bed. "Now, Slavenka, I want you to understand that we are in a very dangerous situation. I am Jewish and so are you, but no one must know, or they will report us to the Germans. Vlad is a Catholic and because we are married, they won't suspect him or me."

She strokes my blond braids. "You look anything but Jewish, but you must still be careful whom you talk to. Say nothing about who you are or where you come from. As far as anyone here is concerned, you are just a visitor. People around here are so afraid of the Germans that if they suspect one little thing they'll report it. And then we are as good as dead. All three of us."

The room has a mirror on the wall. I look at myself and see a skinny runt with long blond braids and a tattered navy-blue dress. Surely that face isn't mine. It is a grey face, with sunken cheeks and black circles under its round green eyes. Babushka's hand gently strokes my hair. I close my eyes and turn weeping into her arms.

Babushka, who comes from Russia, often calls me Slavenka, the Russian diminutive of my name. I love her Russian accent when she speaks Polish, particularly the way she pronounces my name. The sound is like no other. It is soft and melodious. The love she feels for me sounds in the way she says it.

Babushka is short, with very round hips, and large breasts. Her hair is a rusty gold because, I discover, she uses henna once a month. Already in her sixties, she does much physical work around the house and garden, and even carries home large branches from the forest for firewood. She has closets full of silk dresses, but never wears them, because they are too good for Zalesie. Besides, she says, she is saving them for when the war is over. Then she plans to return to Warsaw, to her lovely apartment.

Babushka has a big silver samovar, from which we drink our tea.

In the months that follow, I help Babushka with her chores, and she teaches me Russian. We begin with poems by Alexander Pushkin, the great poet of Russia's golden age of literature. She also reads to me, while translating into Polish, from the Russian novel for young people, *Princess Dzavacha*. I am fascinated with the heroine whose name is Nina. She also had to part with her father and leave her home. She is a very brave girl.

Babushka also teaches me Russian folk songs. I learn to sing "Karobushka" and "Kalinka." We sing and dance together, while Vlad looks on and smokes his pipe. Then, when it is time for bed, she helps me wash up and tucks me in, singing a lullaby.

Even though I go to sleep calm and happy, there are many nights when I have terrible nightmares. I wake up screaming. Babushka comes and takes me to her bed, where I fall asleep while she hums.

There are days, especially rainy autumn days, when I sit at home and just stare down the country road, aching for my parents. The look on Babushka's face tells me she understands.

Sometimes we go shopping. Food is scarce, so we line up for hours to get our ration of bread, one loaf for three days. We usually line up in front of the bakery, and the baker hands out the bread through the window. While in line,

Babushka chats with her neighbours about the weather, and putting up preserves. They pay little attention to me, although from time to time some of them eye me with suspicion.

Our meals are simple and meagre. We eat what Babushka and Vlad grow in their garden: vegetables and fruit in the summer; and in the winter, potatoes topped with cracklings. But we must ration ourselves carefully, or there will not be enough for the three of us. I sit down to each meal only to feel still hungry afterwards. Most of the food is given to Vlad, because Babushka says he is the master of the house. Winter comes bringing ice and snow. Somewhere I had lost my mittens, and my hands become red and chapped from frost. I sit by the frozen window, behind a curtain of snow, fingering the jagged flower patterns of ice. There has been no word from my parents.

Spring arrives and still we hear nothing from my parents. We wonder whether they are still in the Ghetto.

Then comes the terrible month of May, when night after night the sky glows red in the direction of Warsaw. Vlad tells us that the Ghetto is on fire. A handful of Jews refused to be taken away in cattle cars like animals; they are resisting with a few guns and home-made weapons. In retaliation, the Germans are burning the Ghetto block by block.

One night, the sky is so red that the people of our village gather outside their homes to watch.

A neighbour comments, "Look there, the Yids are frying,"

and laughs. I look at Babushka and see the horror in her eyes. Here in this peaceful village, I feel on this night as frightened as I had felt in the Ghetto.

Later, I lie in bed and think about the way the neighbour laughed at the suffering Jews. I picture the Jewish fighters shooting down the enemy: they fall one by one, and the ignorant neighbour is among them. I can go to sleep now, feeling proud that a handful of Jews had the courage to spit at the devil.

CHAPTER 8

"Liar!"

(ROCKVILLE, ONTARIO, 1947)

AT THE END OF THE summer, we moved again, this time to a small town in Ontario so that we could all learn English. I was sorry to leave Marie, my first Canadian friend.

The trip from Ste. Adèle to Rockville was long and noisy. We passed immense stretches of farm land, pastures with grazing cows and grass fields filled with wild flowers. The air blowing in through the open windows was hot and scented with the grassy smell of earth. An hour after leaving Ste. Adèle, Father, who consulted the map regularly, announced that we were in the province of Ontario.

I thought that being in another province would change

the landscape, but it continued on as before. Our bus stopped briefly in the town of Cornwall, let some people off and drove on to Rockville.

After getting off at the bus terminal in the centre of town, we found a taxi to take us to our lodgings. The downtown area was small, with rows of low buildings on either side of a main street. We passed by a movie theatre, a large food market called Schmidt's and Woolworth's department store. We were out of the downtown in three minutes, and that included a long stop at a red light. It was only a few more minutes until we arrived at a rundown section of town, and stopped in front of our new address.

This was very different from the Westmount house, or the *pension* in Ste. Adèle.

The house was painted three different colours. The bottom part was a faded blue, the top part a dirty white and the porch was brown. There were different coloured curtains in each window. Some were half-closed, some all the way. The windows were open, and someone was shouting in French.

We gathered our belongings and walked up the sagging stairs to the door.

When Father knocked, a stout woman with frizzy hair came out and invited us in. The front room reeked of fried onions and burned grease. Father introduced us in his careful European French. The woman, who in turn introduced herself as Madame Gilbert, smiled pleasantly, and offered to show us the part of the house we were to rent.

She led us outside through an unkempt lawn to a door on the side of the house. It opened onto five stairs descending to a kitchen, which had a hot plate, small fridge, table and four chairs. Next to a small dirty window was a narrow bed with a table and a lamp. The adjoining room was furnished as a bed-sitting room, and had a crib in it as well. Finally there was a small washroom, with a yellowed bathtub, sink and a grimy toilet.

Madame Gilbert excused herself and returned to her part of the house. My parents didn't like our lodgings, but it was only to be for a short while, and we had survived worse than this. So they decided that I would sleep on the bed in the kitchen, while they and Pyza would take the bedroom.

I looked out the kitchen window, and saw a creek bordered by tall grass and cattails. I liked the view.

After we settled in, Father bought the English *Rockville Daily* and found an advertisement for English language instruction. Both he and Mother began their twice-a-week, two-hour English lesson, while I watched over Pyza.

As the final days of summer passed, I spent a lot of time on my own. In the evenings I listened to both the French and the English radio programs, and found that I was beginning to understand English a whole lot better. Also, Father made me learn the vocabularies of his lessons.

Outside the house, just at the beginning of the grassy area, near the creek, I found a curious hole in the ground, similar to the one in Babushka's garden where Vlad had tried to grow tobacco. It was deep and overgrown with weeds that grew around a stunted tree whose gnarled branches spread out over the opening. The hole was deep enough for a small person to hide in. With the branches for protection, it felt cosy and safe. I went there everyday to write in my diary, which I kept buried in a box in the sand.

Occasionally, Mother sent me to the grocery, two blocks down the street. One day the grocery had a "closed" sign on the door so I decided to walk to another store. I turned into the street, along which our taxi rode that first day, and walked and walked without any luck.

After half an hour I came to the downtown area, where the main intersection was busy with Saturday shoppers. There was a bank on each of the three corners. The movie house was showing "Night and Day," and I wished I had enough money to see it. But I just had enough for a loaf of bread, butter and tea, so I kept walking till I came to Schmidt's supermarket. It had rows upon rows of grocery-packed shelves, and it took a while to find what I wanted.

The store buzzed with people who spoke mostly English. I felt conspicuous. Did the people around me notice I was a foreigner? I was nervous when the time came to pay. Would I understand what the cashier said? At the checkout I showed her the money and she gave me change. We exchanged no words. I walked back through the side streets near the supermarket. The houses here looked much nicer than the ones in our area. They looked freshly painted and their lawns were like green velvet. I looked into the windows wondering about the lives inside.

When I got home, Mother was upset with me because I'd been gone longer than ever before. Father told me never to disappear for so long without letting them know, at least by telephone.

I asked Mother if I would have to be called "Elizabeth" in school.

"Yes," she replied, "it's a very nice name."

But it wasn't. I hated it. I would feel strange as Elizabeth, and not Slava. I was beginning to feel a split in myself already. Slava on one side, and the wretched Elizabeth on the other.

Monday morning. I felt the old growl of fear in my stomach as I stood with my father in line at the principal's office. I looked down my sweater, skirt and shoes. They were far from new. I didn't have many clothes, and none that were pretty.

Just as our turn came, the shrill bell rang. The secretary looked up at us from her papers and said, "It is nine o'clock This girl will be late for class. What grade is she in?"

Father had prepared some English phrases on a piece of paper, and tried to explain that this was why we had come to see the principal.

"We do not know what grade Elizabeth is in," he answered the secretary.

It was the first time I'd heard Father call me Elizabeth. It sounded so unnatural.

At this point, the principal came out of his office and

motioned us in. He was grey-haired, with a long thin nose and round glasses.

"My name is Dunshill," he said jovially. "What can I do for you folks?"

"I am Stefan Lenski," replied Father. "And this is my daughter, Elizabeth. She is fourteen years old, and has not been to school because of the war in Poland, except for six months afterwards. She can read, speak and write some Polish and French but not much English." He spoke with difficulty, but confidently. I almost understood all he said.

Mr. Dunshill took a sip of coffee.

"I will try to place Elizabeth in grade nine," he said slowly, "but I don't expect that she will pass into grade ten, considering what you have told me. It is already late; I will take your daughter up to her classroom now."

Father thanked him.

"You're in good hands now," he said to me in Polish, and left.

While I sat quietly, dreading the trip to the classroom, Mr. Dunshill wrote something on a piece of paper. Then he picked up his coffee, which he slurped all the way upstairs. In front of the door to a classroom, he handed me the piece of paper.

"Give this note to the teacher," he said, still gulping his coffee, and left me standing alone by the closed door.

I opened the door very slowly and stepped just inside. There I stood for a long time until the teacher finished what she was saying. She beckoned me to the front of the room. I gave her the note, all the while feeling miserable standing in front of the silent class while she read it.

"Elizabeth is a new girl to our school. She has come from Poland and doesn't speak much English, but we hope with our help she will soon learn, don't we? Class, meet Elizabeth Lenski. She will sit over there," said the teacher, pointing to a desk.

A murmur swept the room, followed by a shuffling of papers and the swish of bodies turning as I walked to my desk. I lowered my head unable to meet anyone's eye, and stared at the first page of an empty notebook.

The teacher resumed the lesson and everyone else took notes. I listened but understood nothing. Although I knew a few of the words, I could make no sense of the teacher's sentences.

The bell rang, and the teacher stopped talking. For a moment all eyes turned in my direction. I was being examined. A few of the boys and girls came up to my desk with an inquisitive look. They tried to explain that right now was "recess," a morning break.

I understood some of the questions they asked.

"What did you do in Poland?" asked a pretty girl with dark curly hair.

"I go ballet school," I answered, trying to sound important.

"What did your father do there?" asked another.

"He is important man in government. We . . . family of Russian aristocratic," I managed.

They looked intrigued.

One said, "Aristocratic! What's that?"

Another said, "You know, kings and queens and princesses and counts, stupid."

A blond girl poked her face into mine, jeering, "A princess, eh?"

All I could do was nod.

"When I know English, I tell you," I answered, amazed that I could have said this much.

"You aren't dressed like a princess," said a tall boy eating a chocolate bar.

"Where do you live?"

I didn't answer. I couldn't.

The group started to laugh and ran out of the room, following the boy with the chocolate bar. I was left alone in the classroom, trying to hold back the oncoming tears.

"Don't cry," spoke a gentle voice.

I looked up and saw a tall, dark-haired boy standing beside me. His dark brown sweater matched his eyes.

"Would you like me to help you with these notes?" he asked, pointing to his notebook. "You can have them to copy, if you like. By the way, my name is Joshua." He seemed very kind.

"Thank you, I want notes," I said.

He placed them on my desk. "You can work on them at

lunch or take them home. Come on, I'll show you the playground," he said cheerfully. Thankful, I followed Joshua outside.

The rest of the day passed in a blur of teachers, students and English sentences. I went home with a pile of new textbooks and notebooks. Math, biology, English grammar, history and French. It seemed impossible to learn so much.

After dinner I told Father that I knew nothing about math. There was homework assigned, and I was panicking.

"Don't worry, I'll help you," he promised.

Father explained the math problems, then told me to go ahead and try the exercises on my own. I couldn't do them. I understood nothing. I bit off the entire end of my pencil in despair.

A little later, Father looked at the exercises I had tried to do.

"You didn't understand a word I said," he shouted impatiently. I ran into the bathroom, locked the door and cried in utter humiliation. After I quieted down, I realized that I had cried twice in one day. What was happening to me?

When I came out, Father apologized.

"You can't be expected to learn everything in one day," he said.

I tried to copy Joshua's notes, and do some reading. I couldn't understand much, and working with the dictionary took hours. Finally I attempted some French grammar, and had more success.

At night I kept waking and dreaming. English words echoed in my head.

I woke in the morning feeling tired and cold, despite the warmth of the apartment. As the routine of dressing and eating breakfast progressed, thoughts of school became more and more terrifying. I walked to school slowly but arrived at class on time, slipping quietly into my seat. I didn't dare look at anyone, until I heard a voice calling "Hi, Liz."

I turned around and saw Joshua walking towards me. I didn't answer until he said it again, and then realized that "Liz" must be short for Elizabeth. I liked it better.

I returned his notes, and the bell rang. Lessons went on, and I struggled to understand. At lunch time Joshua helped me again with his English notes. When the bell rang and the French lesson began, I felt happier. I looked over at Joshua. He smiled at me, and I smiled back.

Turning away, I met the eyes of the blond girl who had questioned me yesterday. Later on, she came over and introduced herself as Eva Schmidt. It was hard to talk, and I could see her growing impatient with my inability to understand what she was saying.

I couldn't carry on an English conversation with anyone at school except Joshua. He patiently continued to help me with English grammar. I practised my daily English conversation with him, and was getting better. But every time Joshua and I were together, I would see a peculiar look on Eva's face as her eyes followed our every move.

After a month of struggle, I gave up on my school work in all other subjects but French and English. Not that I didn't listen to lessons and try to participate in class activities, but I gave up worrying about passing into other grades. My parents were preoccupied with other matters and left me alone.

As my English improved, I began to answer the students' questions about who I was and where I came from. But I was still afraid to tell anyone the truth about myself.

Instead, I told them stories about my favourite heroine, the Russian Princess Nina Dzavaha, as if they were the stories of my life. I changed her place of birth from Georgia in the Caucasus Mountains to the Polish Tatras. It was exciting! I became the brave Polish princess who rode her swift black stallion in the valleys of the Tatra Mountains. Persecuted by my royal father's enemies, I went into the mountain caves to hide.

No one objected to my stories, and even Joshua listened with interest. But I was frightened that someone would challenge my lies.

One day Eva came up to me in the corridor.

"We both have blond hair just like princesses," she said pleasantly. "Won't you have a soda with me after school? We'll walk to the drugstore downtown. How about it?"

I should decline, I thought, but my curiosity made me say, "Tomorrow we go. I ask my parents today, O.K.?"

"O.K., tomorrow it is."

That evening I told my parents that I would be home a little later than usual because I had found a nice girl at school who wanted to be my friend. They were very pleased.

The next afternoon over a soda Eva made me nervous.

"Your stories sound like something out of a novel. Where were you in Poland during the war? she asked with the same look of suspicion I had seen before.

"Some lives are unbelievably terrible," I replied, unwilling to bare my soul to her. Besides, she would not believe the real story either.

Suddenly she changed the subject.

"By the way, what does your father do?"

"He is a lawyer. What does your father do?"

She glanced at me as if surprised that I didn't know.

"My dad owns Schmidt's Supermarket, and he is the chairman of the school board," she said proudly. "Did you know that your friend Joshua is a Jew?" she asked, placing great emphasis on "your friend."

I said nothing but stirred my soda.

"My father says that Jews are liars and schemers. If I were you, I'd stay away from Joshua. Jewish people are not popular in Rockville. Most of us here are Christian. Joshua and his parents never mention their religion, but everyone knows that they keep kosher by bringing their food in from Montreal. They never buy meat at my father's store," she said, as if this were a crime.

Then she added, "Say, why don't you come over for supper tomorrow night? My father says that if you are from Poland you must be Catholic."

I could hardly speak. I didn't want to say no, but the way she spoke about Joshua and the Jews made me angry. Yet I was afraid to tell her I was Jewish too.

"I ask my parents. Tomorrow morning I tell you," I said, collecting my books.

After supper I crept into my pit, searching for an answer to my dilemma. But none came. Could it be that Jews weren't liked in Rockville? Wasn't this supposed to be a free country where people of different races lived in peace? Wasn't that why we came to Canada?

Before bed, I asked my mother if I could go to Eva's house for supper. She wanted to know more about Eva's parents. I told her that Eva's father was an important person in town, and she consented, but reminded me, "Just remember to keep our family matters to yourself." There it was again.

"Why do people hate Jews?" The question burst out of me unexpectedly.

"Why do you ask such questions?" Mother said, looking puzzled.

I didn't give up.

"Why does our being Jewish have to be a secret?" I asked.

"Mother is still afraid for us, because as Jews, we have suffered so much." My father's voice answered. I hadn't known that he was listening. He was sitting in a chair by the window in the evening dusk.

"A minority always has to struggle harder to survive," he continued. "When I went to school in Warsaw, I had a teacher who deliberately tried to make me fail. He picked on me constantly even though I was an 'A' student. One day I threw a bottle of ink at him and almost got expelled from school. But our family was rich and money speaks." Father sighed and went on.

"To survive you need money, but you also need an education. That is why you must strive to become educated, no matter what. I struggled hard in order to become a successful lawyer in an anti-Semitic country, and I succeeded. All that success collapsed overnight when the war began. But that was Poland. You should not have to keep your Jewishness a secret here."

Mother turned on the light, and I suddenly noticed how pale and tired Father looked. He grew silent and returned to his reading, holding onto his side.

"What's wrong with Papa?" I asked Mother in the kitchen.

"He has not been feeling well lately," she replied. I sensed that she wasn't telling me everything, but I had other questions to ask.

"Mama, what's kosher mean?"

"Questions, questions," she snapped. "It means that if you're Jewish you shouldn't mix meat with milk, and you shouldn't eat pork. During the war we were lucky to get anything to eat, let alone worry about whether or not it was kosher. And now please go and do your homework!"

I finally understood. Although we were Jewish we did not

keep kosher. When we ate chicken we always put butter on our potatoes. It made me realize that I didn't know much about being Jewish, except what I had learned in the Ghetto.

The next morning I dressed carefully for my supper at Eva's. I was as uneasy after my conversation with her as I was curious to see how other people in the town lived.

When I got to school, I told Eva that I could come to dinner, and she telephoned her mother to let her know I was coming. We promised to meet in the playground at four o'clock.

In school that day, as usual I sat through a math lesson I did not understand. During the French period, however, we had a quiz, and I scored the second highest mark. The teacher shook her head in bewilderment as she collected our papers.

"If you could only do as well in other subjects," she said with a half-smile.

At lunch, Joshua was sitting in the corner of the cafeteria eating his sandwich. I remembered what Eva had told me about him. He was somewhat of a loner, but he certainly didn't look like a liar or a schemer.

I wanted to sit beside him but felt shy. Suddenly he looked up and waved. I went over and sat down without saying anything. I wanted to know more about him, his home and his parents. I didn't dare approach the subject of religion, or anything else personal. Why not invite him over to our place one day after school for tea? When I did, he gave me that warm smile of his and said he would gladly come.

Sitting next to him that day felt somehow different. All the times before he was just someone who took pity on me. Today I felt flushed and embarrassed, and wondered if he thought me pretty. I didn't dare to ask. Instead, I asked him if he liked reading books.

"I've read some Mark Twain and Dickens. I was particularly interested in *David Copperfield*. He had a difficult childhood." Joshua paused, then asked, "Did you have a difficult childhood?"

"Very difficult," I replied, afraid of being questioned.

"Even as a princess?"

"Yes," I said seriously, "even as a princess."

The bell rang just in time.

I saw Eva glaring at us as we stood up. She bent over and whispered something to the girl next to her. I felt my ears burn, as if Joshua and I were doing something wrong.

At four o'clock sharp I was waiting in the playground. Eva came a few minutes late, all hot and sweaty, saying she had just come from a basketball try-out. We started walking.

"That Joshua, he thinks he is the cat's meow. He practises day and night at the basketball hoop. No wonder he is on the school team. I just about got on the girl's team today, but the teacher said I need more practice. I just don't have the time to practice as much as he does, with all the homework and everything."

"Joshua's good in all subjects. Sports too," I said.

"Big deal. How come you and he are so chummy?" she

asked derisively. "Is it because he does your homework for you?"

I was choking with rage, but we were already walking up the path to her house. A tall, blond woman greeted us at the door.

"Come in, come in. I have heard so much about you," she said taking our school cases and putting them in the closet. "Eva, please take Elizabeth to your room while I finish dinner." The house was big, with a square entrance hall and a staircase leading upstairs. I glimpsed a spacious living room on one side, and a formal dining room on the other, similar to the one we'd had before the war. Upstairs, Eva's room was full of dolls from different countries. There was even a doll from Russia. Then she took me to another room, like a study, but without many books.

Hanging on the wall were a rifle and a pistol. Both reminded me of the ones I'd seen the German soldiers carry. I remembered the soldier who pointed his rifle at me the day we were thrown out of our room in the Ghetto.

"What's this?" I asked, suddenly feeling very strange.

"Oh, the rifle belongs to my dad. He loves hunting. See," she said, pointing to a stuffed moose head above the fireplace. She touched the rifle gingerly. "You can touch it too."

"I don't want to touch it," I said and looked at the moose. It had a stupid look on its face. Its eyes were like plastic beads and should have been closed. Then my eyes went back to the pistol. Eva was quick to notice.

"This belongs to my uncle Horst. He is visiting us from

Germany. You know, he tells stories that are almost as good as yours."

"What about?" I asked. It was an effort to speak.

"He was an officer during the Second World War, when the German army captured Kiev. Germany lost the war, but my uncle thinks that Hitler was a great leader who tried to save Europe from Communists, gypsies and Jews."

I felt like throwing up. Why did I come here?

"What's wrong?" asked Eva.

My stomach heaved.

"Where is your bathroom?" I managed.

She pointed to a door down the hall. I walked away slowly.

I locked the bathroom door behind me and leaned over the sink for a moment. I didn't throw up but sat down on the toilet thinking with horror that I was among people who admired Hitler and hated Jews. What to do? I had to go through with the dinner. Mrs. Schmidt was calling us, so I walked back to Eva's room, preparing my act.

Eva led me into the dining room and sat me down next to her. Just then two men walked in. They were both of medium height, fair and heavy-set.

Eva introduced me.

"This is my father and my uncle. Papa and uncle Horst, this is my school mate, Elizabeth Lenski. She doesn't speak much English, and she is from Poland."

The two men bowed and sat down. They started speaking German to each other and I heard the word *Polnische*.

Hearing this language again, after all that had happened, made me shudder. I remembered what the German soldiers did to the city of Warsaw and to our family.

"Papa, Elizabeth is really a Polish princess. She says that she rode wild stallions in the Tatras, and was pursued by bandits, and had to hide out in caves till her father's regiment rescued her."

I tried to keep from trembling.

They all looked at one another, and Mr. Schmidt said, "Is that so?" His "s" sounded like a "z."

But the conversation went no further, because Mrs. Schmidt set the platter on the table.

"These are pigs' feet," said Eva enthusiastically. All I could see in front of me were blobs of fat.

"And this is *Sauerbraten*, also a German dish," she added, pointing to the second platter set down on the table by her mother.

I put a bit of each on my plate. I managed to eat the *Sauerbraten*, but the pigs' feet were just too sickening. I thought of Mother saying that Jews who were kosher didn't eat pork. Joshua certainly wouldn't eat it.

"Don't you eat pork?" asked Mr. Schmidt.

I started to shake my head to say no, then decided to explain that I wasn't very hungry.

The two men spoke German to each other again and laughed. This time I heard the word "*Juden*," the German word for Jews.

"You don't eat pork? Why?" asked Eva. I looked at the two

men, who continued to converse in German. They seemed to ignore Eva and her mother.

"You understand German?" I asked Eva, evading her question.

"No, I was born here. So was my mother. Only my father was born in Germany," she replied.

After supper Mr. Schmidt offered to drive me home and asked Eva to come along. I gave him the address. When he pulled up his shiny car in front of our rickety house and let me off, Eva was strangely silent. I said "Thank you" to both of them and ran into the house.

"How was it?" asked Father.

"It was just fine," I lied. I wasn't accustomed to lying to my parents, but I was getting better at it all the time. I couldn't talk. Only my diary would learn how I really felt, and I had to wait till they went into the bedroom. In the dark, I snuck out to my hiding place. I dug out my diary, brought it into the house, and poured out my heart.

When I came to school the next day, only Joshua and his bright smile helped me through the morning. I glanced at Eva sideways during math class. She didn't look at me at all, and at recess she ignored me. I went up to her — more from curiosity than feelings of friendship. She was sitting at a table alone drinking a Coke, when she burst out, "You're a fraud. My father said so. You're not a Polish princess. My uncle said that stories like yours were made up by Jews during the war to fool people. You're a liar!"

I turned around and walked away. The situation was getting out of hand. What to do? All week I watched Eva. She never spoke to me, but I saw her talking to the other classmates, whispering and pointing at me. Something strange was happening. I wanted to tell Joshua, but he left with the basketball team for Cornwall on Thursday.

Friday I walked home after school as usual. When I arrived at the main street leading to our house, I heard laughter behind me and noises. I turned around.

Walking behind me was a large group of boys and girls. They were all from my class. Why were they following me? What did they want? I started walking faster. Then I heard them calling, "Liar, liar!"

I started to run. I ran towards the house and around to the back and jumped into my hiding place. The gnarled branches of the tree tore my skin, but I gritted my teeth. I pressed myself against the earth, hoping desperately it would save me. As it had done before . . .

CHAPTER 9

The Pit

(ZALESIE, POLAND, 1943)

I AM TEN.

Autumn has arrived in Zalesie clothed in plumes of yellow, orange and red. The trees bow, heavy with ripe fruit, and the golden fields are in harvest. The village becomes noisier. People trade potatoes for flour, fruit preserves for lard, and bargain for all the other things they will need for winter.

I know my way around by now, but I've been told not to talk to strangers and to be seen by the villagers as little as possible. Most of the time I don't come across anyone in my wanderings, and when I do they pay no attention to me.

There seem to be very few children in Zalesie.

One day I wander off across a field to the other side of the village, following a path through the tall grass. At the edge of the field I hear a rustling noise and stop. By the roadside, holding a little dog in her lap, sits a girl slightly older than me.

"Hello there," she says pleasantly.

I say nothing, but she smiles and says, "My name is Irka. What's yours?"

"Nina," I reply. Then I remember that my new name is Irena.

"That's a lovely name. I don't know anyone called Nina," says the girl. "Come on over to my house. It's just down the road."

Irka has an angelic face, with blue eyes like forget-me-nots, and white-blond hair. I feel shy. With no one to play with for such a long time, I don't know how to act. Besides, I was told not to talk to anyone. But she seems so friendly.

"Come on, don't be afraid," says Irka. She gets up from the ground and takes my hand. Wordlessly, I follow.

Her house is white on the outside, and has white lace curtains in the front windows. It's the nicest I have seen in the whole village, and is surrounded by a garden. They even have a clump of sunflowers growing in one corner.

Irka pushes open a heavy oak door and we step into a large foyer. The floor is covered with a ruby-flowered rug.

We go straight to Irka's room and sit down at a little

white table. In the centre of the table stands a miniature china tea service for four. It is the most delicate thing I have ever seen.

A plump maid with flushed cheeks rushes in with a tray. She has a crown of braids on her head and wears a black dress with a white lace apron. She asks Irka whether she wants to serve the lemonade and cookies herself. Irka nods and gracefully pours the lemonade into the china cups.

Out of the corner of my eye, I busily examine her bookshelf, and discover that she too has the Polish version of *Princess Dzavaha*. I take it off the shelf.

"Have you read this?" I ask.

"No, I haven't," replies Irka. "You can borrow any of my books you like."

Wonderful! at last I will be able to read new books. But how will I explain them to Babushka?

"What's your last name?" asks Irka.

There it is, the question I was dreading. My new last name! What is it? I try to think of it, but it won't come.

"Dzavaha," I reply hastily.

"But that's the name of the book you have just shown me," says Irka looking very surprised.

How can I get out of this mess? I say the first thing that comes to mind.

"Well, there is another volume of the book called *Second Nina*. After the first Nina disappeared, there was another child born in the royal family, and they called her Nina also.

It's a true story about my family."

"You mean . . . you are a princess?" Irka asks in a whisper

"Yes," I say, my heart beating like a drum against my ribs. It isn't a complete lie: there is a book called *Second Nina*, and I can see that Irka doesn't have it on her bookshelf.

"I escaped from Russia to come and live here," I continue. "But you mustn't tell a soul because if my guardians find out that I told you, they will punish me severely."

"I won't tell, I promise," Irka whispers, her blue eyes shiny as marbles. "I have never read the story. Would you tell it to me," she asks with a mouth full of cookie.

"Well," I start uneasily, "it's a long story. I was born in the Caucasian Mountains in Georgia, south of Russia. I rode wild horses at the age of six, and when I got lost in the mountains, I survived by hiding in caves. My father, the prince, eventually found me and brought me home. Soon afterwards, my father was threatened by a group of bandits. So he sent me to Poland to live, until it was safe to return . . ."

I don't know how to finish it.

I am getting deeper and deeper into the lie.

"I must go now. Remember, it's our secret," I say.

"Will you come again tomorrow to the edge of the field?" asks Irka.

"Yes," I answer, feeling terribly uneasy.

I borrow *Little Women* and walk home. I feel guilty but at the same time I am happy to have found a friend. With the book hidden inside my cardigan, I enter the house and sneak it under my pillow, then I read it half the night by candlelight.

The next day I go back to the edge of the field. Irka is waiting.

"Tell me more," she says.

I begin to create more details, continuing the first story. I make it very exciting, full of captures and escapes. It's easy, and so much more enjoyable than my life here in Zalesie. And besides, it stops Irka from asking questions.

A week later, on my way to our usual rendezvous, I see five children crossing the field. I didn't know there were this many children in the village. They sit down under a tree and wait for my approach. As I come near, Irka jumps up, claps her hands and shouts, "Here she is. You'll see for yourself who she is after you hear the stories."

I feel frightened. Wasn't the story-telling supposed to be a secret? On the other hand, being popular all of a sudden is exciting. One of the children cries out, "Are you really a Georgian princess? Can you speak Georgian?"

"We spoke Russian in our household," I reply, and sing to them the happy Kalinka song that Babushka has taught me. I dance and clap my hands, then make them clap theirs. The children laugh, and seeing their delight, I don't feel so guilty anymore.

"The children promised not to say a word to their parents," says Irka after they all leave. It is useless now to rebuke her.

These meetings continue into October, when it starts to rain. The children disappear but my friendship with Irka continues. We meet almost everyday, even when it rains. Babushka becomes suspicious, and asks where I go. I tell her that I just need some fresh air.

One morning, Irka doesn't come to the edge of the field, so I decide to go to her house. There are many people milling about on the road in front.

I hear crying and screaming coming from the window upstairs. I poke my head through the doorway and see two bodies covered with white sheets, lying on the ruby-flowered rug. Someone is saying that Irka's parents have been murdered.

For a moment my own parents flash before my eyes. I must go to Irka. I must help her!

I am about to step inside the house through the crowds when I see two German soldiers coming down the stairs. I make up my mind to wait behind the open door until they come out and then make my way to Irka, when suddenly I am pulled from behind, lifted up and carried away. It is Vlad. He carries me in silence.

At home Babushka is waiting at the window. Vlad tells her where he found me.

"Why were you there?" she asks.

I tell her about my friendship with Irka.

Babushka collapses into a chair with a moan. She is terribly pale and has her hand on her heart.

"You are going to kill your grandmother," says Vlad

angrily. "How dare you stray from home and make such friendships behind our backs? Irka's parents are *Volksdeutsche*, German Poles, and her father informs to the German soldiers on Jews in hiding. Also on partisan activity. In fact, everything that is happening in the village. Now the soldiers will search the whole village. Did Irka's father ever see you?"

"No, I was only to her house once; no one was there except the maid. Irka doesn't know that I am Jewish." The words barely squeeze through my lips. I feel as though I am to blame for everything.

Both Vlad and Babushka are silent for a moment.

Then Vlad says to Babushka, "Get some blankets and water and food. Slava goes into the hiding place tonight. I don't want her here when the soldiers search the house."

Babushka does as she is told. I wait at the window, hidden by curtains. Each passing moment is filled with the same dread I felt before I left the Ghetto. Through the curtains, I see two people walking quickly down the road. It's Irka and the maid, carrying their belongings. Irka is crying loudly. I want to run out and comfort her, ask her where she is going. But one look at Vlad's face makes it clear that I can't.

"Get back from that window," says Vlad angrily.

I tell myself that Irka can't keep a secret, or she wouldn't have told the other children about me. I am glad that I didn't tell her the truth about who I really am.

For the rest of the day Vlad works in the far back of the garden. Is that where he is going to hide me, right next to the outhouse?

Babushka has a bundle of things ready. She dresses me warmly, sighing the whole time. Then she hugs me at the door as I leave with Vlad. It's dark and chilly outside; there isn't even a moon to light our way. I follow Vlad down the path to the end of the garden. He stops not far from the smelly outhouse.

"This is your hiding place," he says pointing to a hole in the ground nestling in the heart of the thick raspberry bushes. Vlad places a blanket at the bottom and says, "Get in."

I lower myself into the hole. Vlad throws in a bottle of water, more blankets, a pillow and a paper bag containing my book, paper and a pencil. Then he places thick tree branches across the hole, with moss and grass on top.

"Keep warm with the blanket, and try to sleep. I will check on you from time to time. If you hear the soldiers approaching, just keep still and quiet." Vlad's voice from above sounds muffled. I hear his heavy footsteps leaving, and then nothing.

I snuggle up to the pillow trying to sleep. But I begin to imagine all the things that might happen if the Germans find me. They will kill me, and then Babushka and Vlad for hiding me. Or maybe they will take me to those work camps on the cattle trains that Father talked about. Now and then

I hear a voice, a door slamming, barking of dogs. The normal sounds of a sleepy village. But mostly there is silence
that isolates me from everything.

I wake to the rustling of grass. Sunlight trickles in through
the branches and the moss. Babushka with a kerchief on
her head and a rake in her hand bends over the hole. Pushing aside some of the branches, she lowers a bulky linen-
covered parcel from underneath her apron. How wonderful
it is to see dearest Babushka out in this wilderness. The parcel contains bread with strawberry preserves, and milk. It
all tastes so good. I eat while Babushka pretends to rake the
garden.

"Baba," I whisper, "I need to go to the bathroom."

Babushka passes down a jar. "Here, use this so no one will
see you getting out." I do the uncomfortable thing and remember that first morning in the Ghetto.

"I'll be back for lunch, Slavenka, I know how hard this
must be for you, but be brave. Just like the princess Dzavaha,"
says Babushka and goes back to the house.

The hole feels damp and so does my bedding, and the
stench from the outhouse nauseates me. I place a corner of
the blanket over my nose, pick up my pencil and paper and
begin to write my stories about a child lost in the desert.

Later that day Babushka tells me that I must spend one
more night in the hole.

This nightfall is even more ghastly than last night's. I
hear the shrieking of cats, the howling of dogs, owls hoot-

ing in the trees. I envy the people inside their warm little houses, keeping each other company.

I wake up in the morning to the sound of vehicles. The German soldiers must have finally arrived to search the village.

I bury my stories in a small hole I have dug out. Covered in my blankets, I wait silently, expecting the worst.

I hear footsteps approaching, and German voices. They are nearing the hole, pushing the bushes away with sticks. They are almost standing right above me.

I lie shivering while the soldiers examine the outhouse, all the time talking. I can see them through the branches, plugging their noses. One looks down at the hole and kicks one of the branches. But someone calls from the road, and the soldiers turn away. Minutes later, the vehicles drive away. I want to climb out of the hole, but Vlad orders me to stay there a little longer as a safety measure.

At night, Babushka and Vlad come to take me back to the house. When I crawl out of the pit, I can't straighten out for three days. Vlad explains to me that Irka's parents were killed by the Polish Underground for being informers. I never see Irka again.

CHAPTER 10

The Apology

(ROCKVILLE, 1947)

I HEARD THE STUDENTS running around the side of the house. It didn't take them long to find my hiding place. A face flashed above me, and one of the boys yelled, "There she is, the little Jew-girl!"

In a moment I was surrounded by them. They stood in a circle above my head, jeering, calling me names. I looked up at their spiteful faces, and all of a sudden I wasn't afraid anymore. What did they really know about me to criticize me? What right did they have to persecute me here in Canada?

I began to shout at them in Polish.

"You Nazis! You spoiled little brats!" I stood up in the pit, my blouse bloody from the cuts on my arm. With all the strength I could muster I yelled in English, "I am a Jew! I am a Jew! I am a Jew!"

They stood silent. Then my father came out of the house, and they all ran away.

Later, Father phoned the principal, and told him what had happened. Mr. Dunshill was outraged and asked to speak to me. After apologizing on behalf of the school, he said, "You rest up at home during the weekend and come back to school on Monday."

On Monday morning it was as if nothing had happened. I sat at the desk with my arm bandaged up. The class avoided looking at me. Joshua was still away with his basketball team, and I felt lonelier than ever before. But when the bell rang for recess, the teacher made us all sit quietly and wait. Wait for what? I thought. Then Mr. Dunshill walked into the classroom with his cup of coffee.

"Something ugly and cruel has happened in this classroom," he began. "You have been cruel to your classmate. You acted on prejudice and hate."

He put down his coffee cup, and his voice rose. "This is a free land. Remember your anthem, and remember who you stand for when you sing it. In Canada, people have the right to be whoever they choose or happen to be." He paused. There was a complete silence in the classroom. Then he resumed: "I am leaving it up to each one of you to question your own conscience. Why you acted as you did. And what you can do to make sure that such discrimination doesn't happen again. I am leaving each and every one of you to do the right thing, to make the right decision about yourself and your actions."

Mr. Dunshill spoke with the teacher for a moment, then picked up his coffee cup and left.

There was silence in the class, and then the students began to leave the room slowly and quietly. They still avoided eye-contact with me. I wished again that Joshua were back.

I had permission to go home for lunch. When I returned, I found an envelope lying on my desk with my name written on it. Inside was a letter:

Dear Elizabeth,

We, your classmates, want you to know how sorry we are for what has happened. In spite of everything we like you, even if you are not a princess. Your stories are interesting.

Please accept our sincerest apologies.

Your classmates.

When the students began filing into the classroom, the atmosphere was better. Not that I could feel terrific right away, and forget what had happened. But they tried to make amends. A girl came up to talk. Two boys asked if I would have lunch with them in the cafeteria tomorrow.

Back at home I had one of those deep discussions with my

father. I asked him if people were basically good, and only the Germans bad.

Father thought for a moment, then replied, "It is a difficult question you ask, my darling daughter. The Germans have been among the most civilized and cultured people of Europe. Some of the greatest musical composers were German, like Beethoven. And there were great philosophers, writers and poets."

He shook his head sorrowfully. "It is hard to believe that the German people could have brought themselves to commit such crimes as they did under the Nazis. Yet they did. Sometimes people do terrible things, but we must believe that goodness in man will prevail over evil, and that your classmates can learn the difference between the two. The letter certainly proves that they can learn."

I felt a lot better after our talk, and that finally I was able to tell the truth about being Jewish. But as I was helping Mother with dinner, she told me that Father needed medical treatment. A lump had grown in the place where he had been injured during the war. It meant we had to leave for Montreal very soon.

I was frightened both for Father and for us. What would happen to us if Father became sick?

The next day Joshua returned to school. His team had come second at the Cornwall tournament, the best Rockville had ever done. At lunchtime I told him what had happened. He stared at me with disbelief.

"It wouldn't have happened if I had been here," he said angrily. "They probably knew that and did it while I was out of town. These kids do not know that much about the world," he said, chewing reflectively on his sandwich.

"Eva is wrong to have done what she did, no question," he said. "I don't like her, but I try to understand her. Kids with German names like hers were given a hard time at school during the war. They were picked on pretty constantly."

"I can't feel sorry for her, Joshua," I replied heatedly. "What about us Jewish kids and our feelings during the war?"

Joshua grew silent for a moment, then said, "Maybe some-day you can bring yourself to forgive Eva."

I thought of Irka. She had been German, like Eva.

"Maybe someday," I said.

Then I explained the situation at home, and told Joshua I was sorry to be leaving him.

"I'll miss you very much, Liz," he said. "Before you go, I want to invite you and your parents to our house for Chanukah."

I asked my parents, and they accepted. The Chanukah dinner was two days before we were scheduled to leave for Montreal.

It was a wonderful dinner. Joshua's parents were from Odessa. Father spoke with them in Russian, and Mother in English. Because I knew nothing about it, Joshua explained the Chanukah story to me. "Chanukah is the Festival of

Lights," he said. "It celebrates the triumph of the Jewish people over oppressors, the Greeks, who defaced our synagogues and forced us Jews to worship their idols." He told me that, the ritual of this celebration is the lighting of the menorah, the eight-branched candelabra. A new candle is lit every day for eight days, and placed in one of the eight holders. The ninth candle in the holder of the Menorah, acts as a servant who lights the other candles.

After dinner, Joshua took me aside and said, "I want you to write to me, Liz. Promise?"

"I promise. And you will write, too?" I asked.

"Of course I will. I still want to hear more stories about that interesting life of yours," he said jokingly.

On my last day of school, I said good bye to all my classmates, but avoided Eva. I couldn't bring myself to be friendly to her.

Parting with Joshua was the saddest of all. He gave me a small menorah as a parting gift and kissed me on the cheek.

On the bus to Montreal, hours later, I could still feel the touch of his lips.

CHAPTER 11

Makeup

(MONTREAL, 1948)

THE OLD BROWN SUITCASE was getting heavier. In addition to my precious mementos of Poland, it now contained the brass menorah from Joshua and a book about Chanukah. I carried it into our new apartment and took stock of my room.

It resembled a furniture store. To cross it, I had to hop from foot to foot so as not to knock over the frail side tables, or trip against the mouldy edges of the velour couch. I made my way between two china dogs who sat on their hind legs as if waiting for something to happen. The room was stuffy. The air was trapped between the yellow walls and greasy windows, half-covered by heavy drapes grey with dust.

The foul air, the condition of the furniture and a glaring red velvet chair in particular, somehow reminded me of the room in the Ghetto, on Electoralna street.

Nevertheless it was my own room. I would dust it and re-arrange the furniture.

Father's head popped in through the door.

"We've got lots to do but our exploring mustn't wait," he said with a smile. "Let's go to the street and see what's out there. I am certain that this quarter is very different from Westmount."

I put on my jacket and followed Father out the door, for-getting the shabby furnishings of our new apartment. It was early afternoon. The chill of late November was in the air, but St. Laurence street was bustling with people, auto-mobiles, wooden carts and streetcars. Everyone was rush-ing to and fro.

Smells of herring, pickles, and sauerkraut drifted from barrels lodged in the side-street doorways of delicatessens. Some of the shops had the Star of David painted on the glass with the word "Kosher" in large letters. They sold salamis, meats and poultry. Other shops sold fish, eggs and cheese, and had them displayed in the windows or on the counters. Oranges, red and green apples, and onions were piled up on wooden carts, along with potatoes still covered in black earth.

Everywhere the buyers and sellers haggled and jingled

money. Polish could be heard, along with Russian, English, French and Yiddish. French-Canadian farmers sold produce to Jewish housewives.

The bakeries were the best. I could have spent all my time breathing in the smell of freshly baked bread.

There were shoemakers, tailors and cleaners, men selling pots and pans which dangled from their backs. Used furniture and clothing stores were displaying their wares in the wintry street. Old clothing hung on strings suspended between the doorways and the wooden posts. Rickety chairs and tables stood along the sidewalks. The merchants ignored the cold and congregated outside, warding off the chill by drinking glasses of hot tea and lemon, while sucking on sugar cubes — Russian style — just as I had done in Poland with Babushka.

On the corner of the street stood a group of men dressed in black trousers, long coats and black hats. Underneath the hats, on each side of the head, hung long, thin locks of hair. The men also had thick beards and some wore glasses. Engaged in a heated discussion, they moved their hands energetically, while their heads and shoulders bowed up and down.

"These are the Hasidim, a group of very religious Orthodox Jews. They look exactly like those who lived in the old Jewish quarter of Warsaw before the war," explained Father. "I rarely went there, but some Polish Jews never ever ventured out of their quarter. I always thought them to be very rigid, but it does me good to see a Jewish quarter so alive, where people are free to come and go as they please."

Father's comparison of the two quarters, one so alive and the other so totally destroyed, provoked a shocking thought. I stopped walking and clutched his hand.

"Could it happen here, Papa?" I asked.

"Could what happen here?"

"The Ghetto, like in Warsaw. . ." My voice trailed off.

Father didn't answer at first. Then he said, "Why couldn't it happen here? God forbid that it should. But if another Hitler became powerful and preached enough hatred against the Jewish race, it could happen anywhere, I suppose. Look at what happened in Rockville. But the Nazis lost the war, and there are many witnesses to what they did. If the world doesn't forget, then it should never happen again . . . My, we're morbid today." He smiled at me, and arm in arm we continued our walk.

Traffic grew, and darkness came early. It began to snow. The merchants hauled their wares into the shops, and the carts of produce were packed up. I was glad to return home. The delicious aroma of Mother's cauliflower soup, greeted us on the rickety stairway.

Chanukah was still upon us. I placed Joshua's menorah on the dining room table, together with the candles, and wished that Joshua was here to recite the prayers.

My parents discussed the possibility of inviting the Rosenbergs over for dinner, but Mother was concerned as to how they would react to our shabby lodgings. This was resolved when the Rosenbergs telephoned to invite us over to their place.

As Mr. Rosenberg's Cadillac pulled up in front of our old building to pick us up, the difference between St. Laurence street and Westmount became quite clear. But I wouldn't have traded the colour of our street for the boring elegance of Westmount. When we arrived at the Rosenbergs' house, I was even more struck by the difference.

The dining table was set as usual with flowers, silver and china. A large and ornate silver menorah was placed in the centre. As expensively dressed as ever, Ina lighted the candles and said a prayer in Hebrew. That was the part I enjoyed most. Then she spoiled the moment.

"Well, how is our country girl?" she asked condescendingly. "Did you work on the farm?" I wanted to spill cranberry sauce on her camel-coloured cashmere sweater and make it look like an accident, but didn't dare. Instead, I asked her if she could teach me the prayer for the lighting of the menorah.

"I could, I suppose, but I am really busy with school right now. Call me in January," she said.

But I knew I wouldn't. I decided to write to Joshua instead and ask him. I could hardly wait to get home, to light my own candles, say a made-up prayer, and think of Joshua.

December was long and dreary. I spent most of my time listening to the radio. I could understand more and more

English. During the last weekend in December, my uncle Urek came up from New York to visit us. We dined in elegant restaurants several times, while my little sister Pyza stayed home with a neighbour. When my parents told uncle Urek that I would be starting school in January, he bought me a winter coat and gave me some money for school clothes. A very kind uncle.

January came too soon. On the first morning of classes my stomach felt as queasy as it had been in Rockville.

Once again Father and I found ourselves sitting in the waiting room of a new principal, Mr. Patterson.

"What can I do for you, Mr. . . . ," asked the principal after we finally sat down in his office.

"Lenski, Stefan. My daughter, Elizabeth Lenski," said Father, and explained my situation in pretty good English.

Mr. Patterson didn't drink coffee but concentrated a great deal on his pipe, which he was repeatedly lighting. While we sat there, he kept on receiving telephone calls during which he would coo and constantly smile. As soon as he hung up and turned towards us to discuss me, he would change completely and a stony look would appear on his face. It was like being in the presence of Dr. Jekyll and Mr. Hyde.

"Elizabeth is not the only one with an English problem," said Mr. Patterson stiffly. "Unfortunately, our school curriculum does not accommodate immigrant problems. I suggest that you get her an English tutor outside the school.

Here she will be treated the same as everybody else, and expected to do her best." He then sent me up to a grade nine class with a note for the teacher.

This time I made it to class before it started. The teacher, Miss Bird, showed me which desk had not been taken. Before the lesson began, she introduced me very quickly as "our new classmate, Elizabeth Lenski."

The students briefly glanced in my direction, and the lesson began. This was different from Rockville. Big cities have no time to waste on individuals like me, I figured, whereas small town folk find someone new an object of curiosity. I was relieved, but I missed Joshua. All this time had gone by, and I still hadn't written to him.

"Elizabeth, would you kindly solve the next math problem," said Miss Bird, whose voice seemed to have come from far away.

"Stand up," whispered a freckle-faced neighbour at the desk next to mine.

I stood up. There was complete silence in the room. The hodge-podge of numbers on the blackboard meant nothing to me. I was sure that everyone, including the teacher, thought that I was trying to figure out the problem. But frankly, I didn't have a clue.

Just then the bell rang.

"Well, you may go now, but I'll ask you next time, Elizabeth," said Miss Bird kindly.

I was delighted. My introduction to the class could have

been disastrous. As it was, I overheard girls whispering at the back of the class.

"She looks foreign."

"Yeah, look at her prissy clothes."

At lunchtime the students streamed out of their classrooms and opened their lockers. The corridors began smelling of tuna fish, egg salad, green onions and cheese. There didn't seem to be a definite place for lunch, so I sat down on a book next to the wall and quickly ate my chicken sandwich. Afterwards I fled to the washroom.

The washroom reeked of nicotine as cigarettes were being lit here and there. The girls stood in front of the mirrors, pasting flaming red lipstick onto their puckered lips. Some of them posed, thrusting forward their full chests, their brassieres outlined inside tight wool sweaters.

I was not certain whether I admired or envied them. Standing against the wall, in my navy skirt and white blouse, I felt like a nun next to these sexy creatures.

"Aren't you the new girl?" asked one of the lipstick wearers. "You must be from the old country. I heard that they don't believe in modern clothes over there."

"Lay off, Esther," said a voice from the back of the room. I turned around and saw my freckle-faced neighbour.

The girl called Esther did as she was told, and returned to her cigarette, blowing circles of smoke in my direction.

The freckle-faced girl came up to me. "My name is Miriam. Yours is Elizabeth, right?"

I nodded.

Miriam was of medium height and a bit plump. Her flaming red hair gave her a look of exuberance. She was smiling, not laughing at me, and I liked her.

Miriam was also smoking. Several times she had to pause her frantic puffing in order to cough.

"Sorry, I am not that good at inhaling yet," she apologized. "Would you like to try a Players? They're the latest rage."

I declined politely, and offered her a chocolate wafer with mocha filling.

"No thanks, Liz. Got to watch the figure, you know. They say that big busts are fashionable, but I find them vulgar. I wouldn't mind having one like yours, tiny. You should most definitely accent it with a bra," said Miriam good naturedly.

"Are you wearing one?" I asked timidly.

"Of course. If I didn't, they would be hanging down to my belly button, like an old lady's." We both laughed.

"You have an accent. Where are you from?"

"Poland."

"Must have been hard for you during the war, huh?"

"Very," I replied.

"My parents are from Poland, too, but they also speak Russian. They came here a long time ago, but many of their relatives — my uncles, aunts and cousins — died in concentration camps."

I couldn't say anything. I wanted to tell her about my lost

sister, but my throat felt dry and my eyes were on the verge of tears. So were Miriam's.

"I felt you were a kindred spirit when I saw you, Liz. We'll probably end up being good friends. I must protect you from vultures, like Esther. A rich girl like her can have the moon if she asks her daddy. You'd think that kids who have everything could afford kindness to those who haven't much. Unfortunately, sometimes it works the other way around."

I thought of Ina.

Through the remainder of classes, I tried to make a real effort to understand the lessons. Problems with English grammar were insurmountable, but I felt that I was learning. This was not nearly as bad as Rockville.

After school I followed Miriam to her locker.

"I need my purse, she said, and smiled widely at a boy who had stationed himself right next to her locker. He gazed at her with curiosity, and then briefly glanced at me. I knew that I didn't impress him one little bit.

"Here, look at these." Miriam had turned so that no one could see. She took out of her purse a comb, a lipstick and something wrapped in tissue paper.

"Come with me," she urged, brushing close by the boy whose face went red. "We've got work to do on you!"

She looked at me for a second as an artist eyes his model.

"I am going to nickname you 'Polachka.' That's Russian for 'little Polish girl,' O.K.?"

Back in the washroom, I stood like a mannequin in front

of the mirror, while Miriam did her "work." Several girls watched as she brushed my hair so that it hung over one eye. Then she smeared lipstick thickly over my lips, and raised my eyebrows half an inch with an ordinary school pencil.

"Now let's go into one of the stalls," she suggested.

"Can we come, too?" asked several of the other girls.

"No, my dears, please control your nosey selves for just another moment," said Miriam, shooing them away. She took me by the hand and led me into one of the stalls.

"Take this off," she commanded, pointing at my blouse. Then she took a bra out of the tissue. I took off my blouse and put on the bra, with Miriam officiating at the clasps. This was far beyond anything I could have imagined for a first day at school.

"How does it feel?" queried Miriam, while the girls who crowded around our stall were peeping from below, and chorusing, "Hurry up."

The bra was a little too big.

"I thought so. Since it was too small for me, I was going to return it to the store for a size larger, but if it fits you, you can have it. Or would your mother prefer you to have one that really fits?"

"You don't know my parents," I replied. "They would have a fit if they saw me like this."

"Jailers eh? Don't worry, mine are like that too. We'll break out." Miriam stuffed the cups of my bra with toilet paper.

When we came out of the stall, I looked in the mirror. Although my blouse was looser than a sweater, I could see two small bulges emerging from behind the pockets. Breasts at last! I exalted, feeling the toilet paper rub against my skin. The other girls gathered around. "You look so much more sophisticated now," said one girl.

I looked at myself not knowing how I really felt about this sudden change. After Rockville I didn't trust girl classmates very much. The word "sophisticated" brought Ina to mind again. I didn't want to be like her. How could I be sure that Miriam was really trying to help me, and not make a fool of me?

I ventured to ask her something that I would never have dared to ask before Rockville.

"Are you Jewish?" After all, Poles were also sent to concentration camps.

"She wants to know if I am Jewish! Girls, am I Jewish? Is a Rabbi Jewish? Elizabeth, I want you to meet your classmates, Reva Krantz, Maria Stern, Esther Goldberg, and me, Yenta Miriam Silverman."

With a name like Silverman, she had to be Jewish. "But what's Yenta?" I asked.

They laughed. "It's Yiddish for someone who talks all the time," they explained.

"Now tell us, pretty young blond maiden," said Miriam, "Are you Jewish? You don't look it."

"Of course I am," I answered with a certain amount of pride.

"This school is ninety-five percent Jewish. Didn't you know that?" asked the girl called Reva. How amazing that it seemed to be an almost all-Jewish school.

On the way home, Miriam informed me about the school dances and other social events. The sooner I entered the contemporary ways of fashion and hair style, she said, the sooner my immigrant image will fade.

"Don't worry," she grinned, "we'll have you looking and talking like a Canadian in no time."

As I neared home, I saw Father standing in the window. He saw me and must have gone to open the door as I climbed the stairs. A look of surprise came over his face.

"What on earth have you done to yourself!" he exclaimed.

I remembered that I had gobs of lipstick on, eyebrow pencil, and a hairdo that made me look five years older.

"Papa, I am fifteen years old already. The girls in my class thought I was twelve . . ." Tears began to fill my eyes.

He pulled out a handkerchief and pressed it to my lips. "Look at this!" he said angrily, showing me the red outline of my lips on the white handkerchief. "Is this your claim to maturity?"

"The next thing you'll do is sneak out with boys, and that will lead to God-knows-what."

Now I felt angry. Didn't he trust me? I brushed the tears from my eyes with the handkerchief I still held in my hand.

"Why does my wearing lipstick make you say things like that? Girls here are already going on dates. This isn't Poland!" I said.

"Girls here are spoiled and begin doing grown-up things much too early," he snapped. "Can't you see? They dress and paint their faces to make boys notice them and make passes at them."

"So what's wrong with that? A girl of fifteen starts thinking about boys. In Poland they do it as well, I bet. Only I am sure that they keep it a secret from their parents."

"I don't care what they do in Poland or in Canada, no daughter of mine is going to become a hussy." Father stomped out of the room.

I went into the kitchen, and Mother looked at me with horror. "What have you done to your hair and your mouth!"

All this fuss about a little lipstick, I thought. Mother found a brush and parted my hair in the middle again. I didn't want my hair parted in the middle. Pushing her hand away, I stomped off to my room, and quickly removed Miriam's bra and all the toilet paper fell out. I looked at myself in the mirror. What a mess! I fell on the couch and wept bitterly. That evening I refused to eat dinner; I decided that I disliked my parents.

Later that evening, after I had gone to bed, Mother came in and said that I mustn't worry.

"Soon you'll be older and will do as you please. But in the meantime, watch out for boys. They only want one thing. I've heard that in the high school basements of Montreal, young girls are getting pregnant by the minute."

The next day I returned the bra to Miriam. I didn't feel that it made all that much difference to my looks. And anyway, the elastic band felt uncomfortable.

Right after school Miriam and I went to Woolworth's to buy a lipstick. I chose a pale red. Each day, I would put on the lipstick on the way to school and take it off on the way back, so my parents wouldn't know. They suspected something, however, because I heard Father tell Mother in the kitchen that my lips were always pink, that I was on the road to evil. But he said nothing to me.

In order to brighten my dull wardrobe, I bought two brightly coloured scarves and wore them each in a different way. Miriam said that I was original, but Esther Goldman said I was a show-off. A week later she came to school wearing a bigger and brighter scarf, telling everyone that hers was a "Chanel."

Then one day my world changed again. Father opened a delicatessen. Uncle Urek had been finding it difficult to continue supporting us, so Father had looked around for a business.

I had always been proud of my father. He was a professional in Poland, a well-respected man. Suddenly I saw him selling salami and rye bread. My emotions were mixed. I loved him very much, but I thought he looked pathetically out of place, serving clients over the counter at a deli instead of defending them in court.

Father was hopelessly inept at some things. He wanted each package he wrapped to be perfect. The impatient customer would sigh and pace up and down, waiting for his parcel of herring to be wrapped like a birthday gift. And

Father could not cope with the customer type who didn't know what she wanted, or the rude executive who felt he should be the first in line, while everyone waited.

So I came to his rescue. My afternoons after school consisted of piling bagels and buns in the window, and wrapping parcels of food. When it grew busy, and the language became mostly Yiddish, which Father didn't understand, he would put his hands to his head and run into the back of the store, and I would have to take over. Even without knowing Yiddish I could understand what the customers wanted. Since business was good, I persuaded Father to hire Miriam, who was delighted to earn some money after school.

Miriam's parents were very strict, too, and didn't let boys come near her at home. Some afternoons after school, Miriam's boyfriend, Mark, would come to visit her at the deli. I could see that Father didn't approve, but he said nothing.

They always left as soon as her shift was over. Once I followed them and saw them disappear around the corner, kissing passionately. They didn't even see me watching them. After that, I went back to the store and ate a large sticky bun. The bun was delicious, but I'd rather have had a kiss — not from Mark, of course.

Winter passed and spring was on its way. The dirty snow melted slowly, and the ice was replaced by puddles. The Jewish quarter moved onto the streets again, and I was surrounded by it once more — lively and colourful.

One day, Miriam brought a letter to school, which she

gave me at recess. "A letter from a secret lover, eh Polachka?" she teased.

I couldn't believe it. The letter was from Joshua. He wrote:

Dearest Liz,

You have not written as you promised, so I decided to write to you. By pure fluke, I happen to know Mark Hirsh, who is on your school's basketball team. The team came to Rockville some time ago to play us. We got to talking and he told me that his girlfriend Miriam has a close pal called Elizabeth Lenski. I asked him for your address but he didn't know it, so he gave me Miriam's.

Strange how life happens. But I am so glad to have found you and to know that you have a pal. I am skipping a grade next year so I will be going into grade eleven next fall. After grade twelve, I am thinking of coming to Montreal to go to college.

And guess what! My team will be visiting your school soon. I will let you know when, as I would very much like to see you. Please write to me, and send a photo.

How are your studies?

Affectionately,

Joshua

I wrote to Joshua immediately, and he wrote back. The third letter he ended with, "Love, Joshua," instead of "Affectionately."

I read the letters to Miriam who shared my excitement. Each day I watched for the mail with such anxiety that my parents decided to interfere again. They wanted me to show them Joshua's letters. I refused, took the letters to Miriam, and asked her to keep them for me. I also asked Joshua to write me care of Miriam.

A kind of cold war broke out between me and my parents, and it soon became worse when my spring report card showed that I had failed everything except French and Latin. My English mark was hovering between a pass and fail. My parents told me that if my marks did not improve quickly I would be grounded each night and on weekends so that I could I study harder.

The next morning I shared my problem with Miriam. Then I talked about Joshua for a whole ten minutes. I had never before said so much in one breath, and all in English. I was like a cloud that had been darkening and swelling to the bursting point. In the middle of it, the look on Miriam's face stopped me. Her blue eyes were moist.

"I have to tell someone or I'll die," she said. "I missed my period this month, and I don't know what to do."

The bell rang, the washroom emptied and became terribly silent. I didn't know what to say.

"What exactly does that mean, Miriam?"

"Naive little Polachka," she exclaimed, shaking her head from side to side. "Don't you know what it means? It means that I might be pregnant!"

If someone had hit me over the head I couldn't have been more shocked. Miriam was still a kid like me. To be pregnant at our age was simply unthinkable, unless . . . "Miriam, did you and Mark play a married couple?"

"Finally you got it," she said, smiling weakly. "Your parents did an even better job on you than mine did on me. You have been pretty sheltered."

The next day we played hooky from school. I tried to cheer her up as best I could. She thought she was craving pickles, as her mother had when she was pregnant with Miriam's brother, so I bought her four pickles. These upset her stomach. She cried a lot, too. I had not seen Miriam in this state before. She was always so strong.

At the deli I asked Father if Miriam could come to our house for dinner. He thought that Mother wouldn't mind one more person, and he was right. Mother and Miriam got on right away. After dinner in the privacy of my room, we made a plan. Miriam was going to call Mark. After all, he was half responsible for this mess. She called him from my house and told him to meet her at the deli tomorrow after school.

The next day school was torture for both of us as we could hardly wait to go to the deli. Mark had made himself invisible. Even if he wasn't in Miriam's class, we thought that he might have come over at recess or at lunch. Miriam was beginning to despair.

When we arrived at the deli that afternoon, there was no Mark. "Maybe he's late," said Miriam hopefully, fishing a pickled egg out of a jar. But Mark never showed up. Miriam was beside herself.

Saturday and Sunday I made her go for a walk, and bought

her lunch. She called Mark again but found that he'd gone out of town for a basketball tournament.

On Monday I went to school dreading the state Miriam would be in. When I met her in the hall she was all smiles.

"Guess what?" she whispered.

"You got it!"

"Shhhhh, Polachka. I got it!"

Because of Miriam's close call, my mother's words were beginning to make sense. Fearful for the fate of all woman-kind, I wrote Joshua a letter asking him if he went out on dates.

He promptly replied, "With whom?"

Around that time, Father decided to get out of the deli business. Although he felt completely unfitted for the job, it had been a good source of income. He would have contin-ued, but his illness was growing worse, and that made him decide to sell the deli.

It took Father only two weeks to find a buyer. A Mr. Yan-kelman came to look at the deli accompanied by a rabbi. After spending some time examining the books, Mr. Yan-kelman closed the deal with a sizeable deposit.

On the last day at the deli, I was working as usual when I heard a groan in the back room. I ran back and saw Father bending over the table, holding onto one side. His face was twisted with pain.

I called Mother and she made an appointment with the doctor for that afternoon.

After Father left for his appointment, Miriam and I

worked very hard cleaning the place for the new owner. When Mr. Yankelman came and looked around, he seemed pleased. "You girls have done a good job. Would you want to continue to work here?" he asked.

Miriam and I looked at one another and simultaneously nodded our heads.

"Thank you, Mr. Yankelman," I said, handing him over the keys. That was great news, but my gladness didn't last long.

When I returned home I found out that Father needed to have an operation as soon as possible.

The week of the operation was a struggle. I couldn't go to school, because Mother spent all her time at the hospital. Loyal Miriam brought me my homework each day. I was learning fast that if you didn't do your homework each day, you weren't going to pass the subject. I didn't want to fall behind, but it was hard to concentrate when I had to help out at home. I cooked, cleaned, did the dishes and looked after Pyza. That was good, because I got to know her better. She was three years old, only a year older than Basia had been when she left the Ghetto.

I played with her in the bathtub. Then after supper I sang her songs, and played more games with her. I hoped that by doing these things for Pyza, I'd make up for the way I had treated Basia on the last day I saw her.

Father came home from the hospital in time for a great celebration, which we shared with Miriam's family.

It was May 14, 1948, and Israel was celebrating its forthcoming independence. We all huddled over the radio to hear the news.

There were only two families in the apartment, yet our living room seemed to be filled with people. I felt the presence of shadows from the Ghetto hovering about, listening. It felt as if all of them had gathered here with us. Grandfather, Mrs. Solomon, Sallye, the young teachers, Hala and Fela — and behind them, all the people who died in the concentration camps and on the typhus-ridden streets of the Ghetto. Basia wasn't a shadow. I could distinctly see her dressed in her coat and hat with her arms stretched out towards me.

Mother spoke of all her sisters, nieces and nephews who had died in concentration camps. Father spoke of his father and Basia, and said that the catastrophe which befell the Jewish people during the war remained as much a tragedy for the living, as for the dead.

Why did I survive, I asked myself? Why me, and not Basia?

CHAPTER 12

Victory and Loss

(ZALESIE, POLAND, 1944)

I AM ELEVEN.

After I had almost given up seeing them again, my parents appear in Zalesie. It is a beautiful autumn day, but they seem like ghosts, pale, thin and shabby. Above all, silent. They're tired. I sense their tiredness in the way they greet me. Babushka greets them with exuberance. Vlad offers them his peach liquor and brings out the glasses for special guests, the ones with silver holders.

I sit on Father's knee while he speaks of the last days of the Warsaw Ghetto. "Your mother left the Ghetto with the last truck of Jewish workers who had permits to work on the Aryan side. We planned her escape. A doctor friend on the Aryan side, a Christian, to whom I had sent word, came to her place of work, and took her away on the grounds that she was ill with an infectious disease, and needed medication. They let her go. Then the doctor and his wife hired her as a maid, and she never returned to the Ghetto. We got her false papers, of course. Her name is now Zofia Mlynarska, and mine is Felix Mlynarski. We didn't see one another for six months. During that time I was wounded in the arm and hid in a shelter built by the Jewish fighters. One day the Germans set our building on fire to force us out. Since anything was better then getting caught, I took a chance and climbed into the sewers below the building.

"I walked for a long time not knowing where I was. At various manholes, I poked my head out but each time the smell of the burning Ghetto told me to keep going. The tunnels were full of rats and sewage. After many hours, the stench and my own tiredness were too much for me and I realized that I had to get out. At the next manhole, I lifted myself onto a quiet dark street. By some act of mercy I had escaped the Ghetto.

"Then I went to find your mother. Her friends let the two of us stay with them for several days before we left for the country. We went to a village called Gloskow, where a man, who took us for Christians, rented us a part of his house. We still rent there; the man doesn't suspect that we are Jews."

My father is weary and stops speaking. Mother continues: "After we were settled we thought that we would see Basia first. So we went to Otwock, where she was staying with some friends of ours named Tomas and Anna, a Gentile couple who were childless. We wanted to take her with us, but Tomas insisted that Basia would be safer with them, so we left her."

Mother's face is very sad as she continues. "Tomas has grown very greedy and is now asking us for money. It's like blackmail. If we don't give him what he wants, he will not return the child to us. I don't know how all this will end . . ." Mother can't seem to go on talking.

Babushka suggests that they lie down for awhile. They rest for an hour then leave quietly, saying that they will be back but they don't know when.

Months pass. One day I am sitting by the window on a rainy day, imagining that my parents are coming down the road. Then I see two specks moving along the road. It can't be them. It *is* them.

"They're really coming," I shout to Babushka, jumping up and down. She bids me stay inside, while she goes out to greet them and brings them inside the house. That's where we hug each other.

They don't look as tired this time, but I can tell from their faces that something is wrong. Father doesn't even take off his coat when he begins to speak.

"This morning Tomas came to Gloskow; he told us that

one of their neighbours saw Mother and recognized her from before the war. This neighbour informed the Germans that Basia is a Jew.

"Last night the soldiers surrounded Tomas' villa, and the Gestapo came in to question him. They checked all the papers and insisted that Tomas and Anna bring Basia to headquarters. We don't know how all this will end, and we don't dare go to Tomas' house . . ."

Mother starts to cry.

I run into my room and close the door. I fall to the ground in front of the window and beg God to save my sister.

"Please, dearest God, keep my little sister safe, and forgive me for being so mean, for pushing her away. I didn't mean it. If you save Basia, dear God, I will be the best person, I promise, and I will never, ever, sin again."

I feel spent, but I make a pact with myself that if God listens to me this time, I would never again doubt his existence, as I did the day we entered the Ghetto.

My parents leave after supper, telling me to be patient and wait for their return. Days drag by.

I watch and wait.

God is on trial.

Finally Father comes to Babushka's house. He has aged a hundred years. I have never seen him look like this before, but I know even without his saying anything.

"Basia is dead," he tells us. "The soldiers have taken her away and murdered her." Father struggles to get the words out. "To prove to us that she is dead, Tomas uncovered her grave. I saw her legs, her socks. Her face was disfigured, beyond recognition . . ." Father begins to weep.

"Then you have no real proof that the grave was hers," says Babushka. "Couldn't all this have been staged by Tomas and Anna? Maybe they simply didn't want to give her back to you?"

There is silence.

"Maybe you're right, Mama. Even so, how can I prove it now? Tomas swears that she is dead," says Father.

I want to think that Babushka is right, that Basia is alive somewhere. Will I ever know?

After that I stop saying my prayers for good. God didn't listen, and I am angry with Him for having made us Jewish.

In the spring, Father comes to take me away. I am sorry to leave Babushka, but she is ill. She has fainted several times. Vlad says that it was a mild heart attack. I feel that he blames me for her weak heart.

Father takes me by train to the village of Gloskow.

He holds my hand and explains the strangest thing.

"Listen carefully. In our papers, you are Irena Kominska, and we are Felix and Zofia Mlynarski. From now on you must call us Auntie Zofia and Uncle Felix. We will call you Irenka. No slips must be made or someone may become suspicious and inform on us. We must survive. Do you understand?"

I don't really.

"Do we have to lie to survive?" I ask.

"We cannot tell people who we really are. That could mean our death," answers Father.

The train's monotonous rhythm is putting me to sleep. But Father's watchful eyes tell me to stay alert. A peasant woman with a basketful of cackling chickens sits down near us. She smells of raspberries, even though they are not in season. A man across the isle reads a book, but every so often his bespeckled eyes look in our direction. The woman gets off at the next station.

I think of Basia. Somebody knew who she really was.

I think of Irka, and what might have happened if I had told her who I really was.

For the first two weeks in Gloskow, I don't call my parents anything. I stop talking altogether. I listen and observe. Father has a job in the forest cutting trees; Mother cooks and cleans for the man who owns the house we live in.

Mother tells him that I have just been very ill, and that is why she isn't going to send me to school. He doesn't seem to suspect anything. There seem to be no other children or people around the place.

"Why don't you talk?" asks my mother, who is used to my constant chatter.

"I am afraid to call you Auntie. It's so strange, and what if I forget while the landlord is here?"

"Don't worry, you won't slip, and if you do, I will explain that you miss your mother so much that sometimes you forget I am your auntie."

Little by little I start calling my parents Auntie Zofia and

Uncle Felix. Months pass, and we go about our chores, always tense and careful lest a slip is made and we are discovered.

Mother's stomach begins to look as it did before she had Basia. When I ask, she tells me that she is three months pregnant. I can't imagine having another sister now, in these awful times. I spend my days reading my few books over and over. The pages have become yellow and torn. I sit by the window and stare out at the white world, and daydream.

One winter day, three truckloads of German soldiers arrive and make their camp in the village not far from our house. They wander about, talking, laughing. One even smiles at me, and it sends shivers right through me. If he only knew.

Then one day, the sound of heavy guns can be heard in the distance. The German soldiers speed by our house in convoys of roaring trucks and cars. I am scared, but my parents are strangely cheerful.

"The Germans are losing the war and running," says Father grinning happily. "The Russians will be here soon."

When the news arrives that Warsaw has been liberated, Father decides to go there on foot to find us a place to live. We wait anxiously for his return as the winter days pass.

There is no food in the village. It was all taken by the Germans when they left. Our landlord seems to have disappeared somewhere. I descend to the cellar full of scurrying rats to look through the potato sacks. All I find is a rotten turnip. I throw it to the rats. I return upstairs to collect some old crumbs from the dining table to share with Mother. The thunderous sounds of guns are coming closer and closer. We are so hungry and cold that neither of us has the strength to move. We just lie in our beds.

All of a sudden a stillness descends upon the village. No more thunder. Soon we hear different noises outside: engines, and the voices of men shouting in a familiar-sounding language. It resembles Babushka's language — Russian.

Suddenly our door is flung open, and a tall young man wearing a sheepskin jacket bursts into our room. He has a cap with sheepskin ears flapping about. Seeing us, he breaks into a grin, exposing a set of the whitest teeth.

"*Zdrastvuite dzievotchki*, hello girls," he says in Russian. His black eyes flash at us out of a very dark-skinned face.

Mother gets up from the bed with difficulty. Using a mixture of Polish and mime, she tries to communicate with him. They establish that he wants Mother to cook for the officers of his regiment.

More soldiers arrive carrying chunks of lard, sacks of flour and potatoes into the kitchen. Soon Mother has made a potato soup and dumplings with onions fried in lard.

We eat with the officers in the large dining room. They have vodka, cigarettes and even a bag of candy for me. They toast their victory over the Germans.

Little glasses are filled, refilled, and raised in the traditional Russian toast to health — *Za zdorove*. The men down their glasses in one shot, and there is laughter and song. The young man who burst into our room picks me up and whirls me around shouting "*Krasavitza!*" — that I am a pretty girl.

The room spins.

We are free, free. The horrid war is over. I want to scream "Mama!" But I see the landlord. He must have returned and is staring at us. I trust no one. Perhaps it still isn't safe for people to know our real names.

After the feast, Mother tells me to go and pack my brown suitcase. We're leaving the next day for Warsaw.

The train station is crowded with the Russian army, triumphant with its victory over Nazis. The cars are packed with soldiers and, even though it is January, all the windows are open, filled with heads and waving arms.

"No civilians!" shouts a soldier in Russian, his rifle barring us from entering the passenger car. We hurry from one car to the other and are always pushed away, but we try once more.

"No civilians!" shouts another soldier.

"It's all right, they're with me," says a loud voice from behind. The soldiers move away and make a path for an officer. He ushers us onto the steps, and we recognize him as one of the men who dined with us the night before. The soldiers let us pass. Mother manages her most beautiful smile of gratitude. The officer salutes us and disappears into a compartment, while we sit down on our cases next to the windows. The compartments are reserved for officers, while the corridors and other seats are for everyone else. There are few civilians aboard besides mother and me. The rest are women whose laughing and talking can be heard coming from the compartments.

The train pulls out of the station.

We are surrounded by Russian soldiers, standing up, sitting or lying on the floor. They shuffle about, and mill back and forth practically stepping over us. Some smoke, drink or sleep. A few have their arms or legs in bandages, and moan in pain. The car smells of sweat, vodka, nicotine and blood.

Once it becomes dark outside, the only light in our corridor enters dimly through the dirty glass windows of the compartment doors.

Mother and I sit on our suitcases in a sea of cigarette butts and empty vodka bottles. The soldiers who have been drinking begin to slur their words and fall over each other with silly laughter. Mother keeps her back to the wall of the train. I am scared.

In front of us, the compartment door opens onto the corridor, and our friend, the officer, comes out. He is short and stocky, very dark, with thick black eyebrows. He pushes his way through the litter towards Mother, and addresses her in broken Polish.

"My dear lady, you should not be sitting on the floor in your condition. Why don't you come into my compartment? I have just got rid of the other officers!" He laughs. "Come, come," he urges, helping Mother stand up. She does it with difficulty, as she is now six months pregnant.

"But my daughter must come, too. I will not go without her," says Mother firmly. He looks at me and hesitates, but finally agrees that I can come along.

It is sheer heaven in the compartment. It has soft seats, and I can just sink into them instead of bracing myself up on a little suitcase. Mother sits on the other side with the officer, who moves closer and closer to her. She pushes him away. Even on the opposite side I can smell alcohol on his breath.

"Maybe a little food?" he asks.

Maybe? Mother and I haven't eaten all day.

He brings out a can of sardines, a hunk of sausage and a loaf of bread. We eat hungrily. He moves very close to Mother again, and pours her a glass of vodka. She refuses. He begins to down one vodka after another, and suddenly grabs Mother and starts kissing her. Mother jumps up, grasps my hand and pulls me out of the compartment. We return to our old place. Luckily our suitcases were left alone.

The soldiers are now really drunk. They laugh continuously, pointing at us and at the officer's compartment. After five minutes, the officer comes out again; his face is red and angry. He walks up to Mother and starts touching her. I scream. He recoils. He advances again and I scream louder. He goes back to his compartment, but tries again later. I scream and scream. My throat is on fire, but I must save Mother from this ugly creature.

Eventually half the car is snoring. The officer stops bothering us. The trip seems to take forever; the train stops frequently and stands at the station for long periods of time.

Blessed daylight comes at last. One tired pregnant lady and a little girl with a very sore throat arrive at the Warsaw terminal.

CHAPTER 13

The Ruins

(WARSAW, 1945)

I AM TWELVE years old.

Warsaw is in ruins. Brick, stone and broken glass lie everywhere in the streets. Twisted steel hangs from buildings ravaged by fire and bombs. Staircases dangle in mid-air.

People walk cautiously, for unexploded bombs lurk among the ruins waiting to blow off a child's foot or hand.

Drunken Russian soldiers paw helpless women on the streets. Other soldiers lie wounded in the corners, huddled against pieces of concrete or wood. Some are still bleeding and look half-dead.

The streets are so grotesquely changed that it is difficult even for a Warsaw native to distinguish one from the other.

There are no cabs, streetcars or telephones; only army trucks drive on the roads, while masses of civilians wander on foot. We walk for what seems like hours.

Unable to take another step, I pause and sit on my suitcase. "Where are we going, Mama?" I ask.

"Papa and I promised that if he doesn't return to Gloskow within a certain time we'll meet at our old address on Aleje Jerozolimskie," she replies. "He is supposed to come there every day to look for us. It's not far from the train station, but it's hard to find my way in all this rubble. Just be patient for a little while longer."

When we have rested, we pick up our suitcases and walk on. With swollen and aching feet, we finally arrive at our old apartment building. Amazingly, it still stands, although it is without windows and fire has blackened its walls.

We walk into the courtyard. The once beautiful garden is covered in snow. Father is nowhere to be seen. Mother decides to wait for him in one of the empty apartments overlooking the courtyard. Dusk approaches and we are almost frozen but glad to be off the street. People can be heard roaming around in the building, but no one bothers us. Mother and I huddle together to keep warm. Half asleep, half awake, I hear a noise.

"Here you are, you two! Wake up!"

It's Father, smiling and happy to see us.

"Come, I've got a royal carriage waiting for you outside," he says.

Dazed, unable to utter words through our cracked lips,

we climb into a broken *dorozhka*, which is pulled by a horse. Parts of the side have been gouged, but the wheels are still good. Everything seems different, except the driver with a whip in his hand, and a heavy dark-blue jacket and matching cap with a brim, slanted over a tanned wrinkled face. Just like the one before the war who drove Mother and me to the dressmaker.

"I don't guarantee that he will take us all the way," says Father in good humour. "I found him soon after I returned to Warsaw. He and his horse were starving. I brought them food and drink and persuaded him to come with me." Father climbs up next to the driver, and the horse ploughs through the debris-laden streets for hours. Periodically someone jumps onto the side of the carriage, rides a way, then jumps off.

"The fact that Mama is pregnant justifies our use of the carriage," Father explains from above. "So don't feel guilty." We finally arrive at an apartment building on Lwowska Street, one of the very few streets that were not destroyed.

Father tells us how lucky he was to have met up with some old friends, who asked him to serve in the legal department of the new provisional Polish government. This position has merited him a place to live and money to buy food.

That night, safe in our new apartment, I sleep my first night in freedom. Mother tells me afterwards that I slept for a day and a half.

Four months later, a round-faced baby girl is born. We call her Pyza. Mother is quite ill afterwards, so Father hires a hefty girl from the country called Marysia to do the house-work and help with the baby. The presence of a new baby is like the beginning of a new life for all of us. She almost becomes our second Basia, and some of the gloom is dis-pelled.

In the meantime, Warsaw is awakening from her night-mare. Polish people who love their country set about re-storing her to life.

We love Poland and Warsaw, my family and I, just as much as the Christian Poles do. We watch joyfully as order sets in, more and more each day, defying the ruins. The rub-ble is being cleared away and schools open. I start attending grade seven. When I am not in school, I roam the streets, watching the reawakening with fascination. I ride the street-car from one end to the other. The conductors come to know me, and don't even bother to ask for money. Some-times I am accompanied by Marysia, as Father doesn't like me to be on the streets alone, particularly after dark. Mary-sia loves men, and many soldiers stop her on the street. When she goes off with one, she makes me promise not to tell my parents. While she is away, I continue my daily exploration of the city.

The Polish spirit is surfacing. The pulse of the city beats again, and songs are composed in dedication. The Poles sing an ode to Warsaw:

Warsaw, beloved Warsaw
City of hopes and dreams
Oh how I long
To see you again
I'd give up my life for you . . .

At the same time, we begin to learn the tragic truth about the fate of Poland's Jews during the war, as the people emerge from the cellars and attics, and return from concentration camps.

Friends from before the war come to visit my parents. They sit around our dining room table for hours discussing the horrors of Nazi crimes, which they call Genocide. They tell us about their relatives who boarded the trains to the so-called labour camps and never returned. These labour camps were really death camps, they said. When the Jewish people arrived there, all their possessions were taken away and divided into heaps of glasses, shoes, suitcases and other items. Then they were told to undress and take showers. Upon stepping into the showers, they were gassed to death. Millions died that way at camps called Auschwitz, Treblinka and others, where Jews themselves were ordered to dig mass graves.

Someone mentions a familiar name: Dr. Janusz Korczak, the gentle doctor who ran an orphanage in the Ghetto. I still remember him on his balcony watering flowers. They say that Dr. Korczak and his two hundred orphans were put into cattle cars and sent to a camp called Treblinka, never to be heard of again.

Mother has not been able to find any of her relatives. She knows that some of them were sent to concentration camps, and haven't returned.

My parents always send me to my room when these discussions begin. But I eavesdrop. It seems that the war has not ended for the Jewish people.

In the meantime, my solitary excitement of roaming the streets is short-lived. Father forbids me to go out on my own, except to school and back. The streets are dangerous because of pilfering and drunken soldiers.

I hate school. It is boring and monotonous. They make us memorize masses of history, geography and literature straight out of books, then recite these passages word-for-word, without any explanation, discussion or understanding.

I make friends with a pair of blond, blue-eyed, Gentile twins, named Lola and Maryla. Both have brown, decaying teeth that smell awful, the result of an illness during the war. They are bright and kind, and one day they invite me to their house for tea after school. I don't ask Father's permission because I know he will refuse.

The street and the number of the building are easy to find. I open the gate and go through into the courtyard. I cannot believe it. The building on the inside of the courtyard is almost totally destroyed. No one could live here. I must have made a mistake. Then I see the number of their suite on the wall, with an arrow pointing at an apartment high up off the ground. Hanging in mid-air are staircases supported by a wall only on one side.

No elevator of course. That means a climb to the fourth floor. A sign in the courtyard says, THIS BUILDING IS DE-CLARED DANGEROUS AND MAY ONLY BE USED AT YOUR OWN RISK. I debate with myself. I promised to be there, didn't I? I am not a coward. At least I don't think I am. Father wouldn't be afraid if he promised, and neither would Nina Dzavaha, my storybook heroine.

I proceed carefully towards the staircase. It swings as I place my foot on the first stair. What if it falls, with me on it? It continues to sway all the way up, and when finally I reach the top I feel weak with relief. I try not to think of having to go back down.

I am greeted at the door by the twins.

"You made it, brave girl. Come on in," they say.

We sit at the table, while their mother serves us tea and cookies. She is a slight lady, with nervous hands. She doesn't sit with us. We talk for awhile, and the twins tell me that their father went to fight with the partisans, and never came back.

"We don't know whether our father is dead or alive," they say.

Father! the word registers in my mind that I must be home before dark, and here it is getting dark already. I collect my hat and coat, thank them for everything, and take a deep breath. One of the twins laughs. "Don't worry, we do this several times a day. Just take your time walking down," says Maryla, and closes the rusted door.

The building is dark and silent; there isn't even an electric light in sight. With each step I take, the staircase swings and creaks.

I can't see. The staircase seems endless. Something scurries past me. Maybe a rat, or maybe a wild alley cat. My heart is bursting and I can hear it thud. I can't breathe. I miss a step and fall a couple, hanging onto the swaying railing. I hurt my finger on something rough, and upon touching the sore spot with my mouth, I taste blood.

Finally, I step out onto a dark street. From the darkness come noises of men and women laughing. I feel relieved to know that I am not alone on the street. An old lady passes by with a young Russian soldier following behind her. He snatches her bag. She screams and runs into the nearest building. The soldier smiles stupidly as he walks back past me, putting his face up to mine and saying something I don't understand. I break into a run and arrive at the door of our apartment. I am scared. What will my parents say?

I ring the bell and the door opens.

"Where have you been?" asks Father in a stern voice.

"At a tea party, Papa, with some friends from school."

"Did you forget what I said to you?"

"No, Papa, I am sorry, I . . ."

He snatches me by the back of my school tunic and drags me into my room. He throws me on the bed face down, and starts to spank me.

"Where have you been, where have you been, where have you been?" Over and over.

I stifle my pain by biting on a corner of the pillow. I hate him. I hate him. Then it is over. He leaves the room. My head hurts and my bottom smarts.

This wasn't my father, I think. He has never laid a hand on me before.

I sit in the dark bedroom for hours, feeling wretched. Someone knocks on the door. It's Father. He turns on the light.

"I thought that we could all go to a matinee film tomorrow, and then get some ice cream. What do you think?" he asks.

I see it in his eyes. This is an apology.

I nod my head.

That night I hear my parents talking until very late. Mother wants to go to America, but Father doesn't. He worries about how we would survive in a strange country, unable to speak English, and without money. He is already in his forties, and no longer has the energy of a young man. At least here he has a position and a place to live; he feels himself independent. There he would have to depend on his brother-in-law, uncle Urek, who lives in New York.

Mother argues that she is tired of this war-ruined country. How will the Russians treat the Jews? Their leader, Stalin, hates them. Besides, all her family died in Treblinka, and Urek is her only brother left. It's easier to get out of Poland now; later, it might become more difficult. Some of their friends have already escaped to California to start a business with the diamonds they hid in toothpaste tubes.

Nothing is resolved that night. But as months go by I hear other things. Uncle Urek had found us through some agency in New York that searches for lost families in Europe. He writes that he is sending us papers for a visa either to America or Canada. If we want to stay in America, we will first have to spend three years in countries such as Cuba or Canada before we can get permission to live there. Canada is a good place to live, he says, although also difficult to get into.

One day Father takes me to Babushka to say goodbye. Too old and ill, Babushka doesn't want to come. Everyone is crying; it's a sad farewell. Poor Babushka, I'll miss her. On returning home, Father tells me to pack my brown suitcase. I am sad and confused. I don't want to leave Poland.

"Slava," says Father gently, "I am sorry that I haven't discussed this with you sooner. But we are leaving under tense circumstances; the less said the better. We will fly first to Sweden, then leave almost immediately on a ship bound for Halifax. He hugs me and says, "We have a long journey before us. Let us hope that it's our last."

A few days later, I am sitting on my first airplane, watching Warsaw disappear beneath the clouds. Goodbye Poland, will I ever see you again? Goodbye Babushka! And you my little sister, what if you are still alive?

CHAPTER 14

Love and "Love"

(MONTREAL, 1948)

MR. CELLINI, THE Latin teacher, was short and bulky with a mane of grey hair that made him look like a small lion on the prowl. When he wrote on the blackboard or paced up and down eyeing his academic prey, there was no doubt in my mind who was the king of this jungle.

Many of the students in my class who were good in math or science seemed inept at languages. But I found Latin interesting and did well without working hard at it.

One day, Mr. Cellini called Esther Goldberg to the board to conjugate the verb to love — *amare*. She giggled and wrote: *ameo ameas ameat ameamus ameatis ameant.* I think

Esther had a little crush on Mr. Cellini. When he asked the class if Esther's conjugation was correct. I put up my hand.

"It's wrong," I said. "It should be *amo amas amat amamus amatis amant*, without the *e*."

Mr. Cellini asked the class, "Who agrees with Elizabeth?"

Only Miriam put up her hand. No wonder. Who would agree with someone who was failing most of her subjects?

"And how many think that it is spelled correctly on the board?"

All the other hands went up. Esther was stuck-up, but she was also one of the best students in class. Of course, I thought, why not side with her?

The little lion smiled and said, "Well, all of you are wrong; Elizabeth is right."

Not a sound was heard. Miriam gave me a triumphant look, and everyone else looked at me with surprise. For the first time, the name "Elizabeth" sounded good.

Mr. Cellini called me aside at the end of the lesson and told me I was the best grade nine Latin student he had ever had. "Keep it up and you can expect an A on your final re-port card," he said.

Despite Mr. Cellini and the Latin class, things were not going well. Except for French, I struggled with other subjects to no avail, and life was even worse outside of school. Father was ill, and Joshua far away.

One Friday afternoon, just as school ended, Miriam asked me why I looked so glum. I wasn't in the mood for a heart-to-heart, so I said sarcastically, "Why, everything is just pie à la mode!"

"Come on, Polachka, don't give me that," she pressed on. "You're just miserable because your love life is in Rockville."

I had to laugh. I hadn't exactly thought of Joshua as my "love life." Miriam always managed to pull me out of my gloom. Then she asked if I was coming to the dance in the gym that afternoon.

"You need some fun, and the dance lasts only two or three hours," she insisted.

I hesitated for a few minutes, thinking that I wasn't properly dressed for the occasion in my moth-eaten sweater and old grey skirt. Then I said okay and called home to say that I'd be late. Soon, Miriam and I were in the washroom dolling ourselves up: fire-engine-red lipstick, pinched cheeks, slanted eyebrows and eyes half-hidden by hair.

"Not bad," we chorused, as we marched arm-in-arm to the gym. Someone was playing the "One O'Clock Jump" on the piano. The music was fast and frantic.

"Smile, for heaven sakes, or you'll be a wallflower," whispered Miriam.

"What's a wallflower?" I asked, but Miriam had already disappeared onto the dance floor with Mark, with whom she had made up several weeks ago. I soon found out what wallflower meant! For at least fifteen minutes, I stood supporting the wall, wistfully watching the dance floor.

The dancers looked as if they were struggling with each

other. The boys pushed and pulled, and the girls turned and whirled, as they danced the "jitterbug."

I continued to stand alone against the wall, ignoring the laughter and chatting all around me. The gym was decked out in pink, blue and white balloons gently swaying like monster flowers. Matching streamers coiled in the breeze like snakes. In the emptier corners of the gym sat several teachers, surveying the dancers.

I practised smiling, till my jaws felt stiff. When that didn't work, and still no one asked me to dance, I decided to practise something new. I tried catching the eye of a dark-haired boy who reminded me of Joshua. That didn't work either. When he looked away, I decided to hypnotize him mentally into asking me to dance. I concentrated so hard, with my eyes closed, that I almost went into shock when a voice said, "May I have this dance?"

The dark-haired boy was standing in front of me.

"My name is Paul. What's yours?" he said, almost yelling above the din of the music.

"Elizabeth," I replied, feeling awkward.

"Come on, let's jive," he yelled. For the next ten minutes, he pushed, hurled and twirled me until I was dizzy. At one point I fell, and he just stood there and laughed for a moment, before helping me up. He smelled of sweat, and his hair was greasy. On closer contact, he didn't appeal to me at all. His eyes were dull. But I closed my eyes and pretended that he was Joshua.

At the end of the dance, I searched frantically for Miriam, but she was nowhere to be found. Sweaty Paul was following me around.

"Can I walk you home?" he asked, sliding his dirty fingernails through his gluey hair. What will my parents say? I wondered. But I didn't know how to refuse him.

Although we didn't speak much on the way, he insisted on holding my hand. This was a new experience, and my hand felt like a blob of jelly in his. We reached our block, and just as I feared, Father was pacing up and down in front of our building. In the cold, his breath came out in white puffs as he paced.

"What's your name, young man, and where do you live?" he questioned Paul as if he were cross-examining a criminal.

"Paul, sir. I just live two blocks away."

"What were you doing with my daughter?" asked Father, thrusting his face closer to Paul's.

Paul backed away from Father, looking at him as if he were a maniac.

"I was just walking your daughter home from the dance."

Father's face reddened. "What dance? She is not allowed to go to dances. I didn't give her permission to go to a dance. Slava, get in the house!" Then he turned to Paul and said, "My daughter is quite capable of walking home on her own. And if she isn't, she has me to pick her up. You are not needed here."

I was aghast at Father's speech, heavy with a Polish accent.

Paul turned around and began to walk away.

"It's dark out, Papa. I didn't want to walk alone. We only walked," I explained. Father didn't seem to be listening. Instead, he lifted his hand and slapped me across the face, and then again on the other side. The hot pain sent a current of rage through me. But I said nothing and followed Father into the house, like an obedient servant.

We ate dinner in silence, except for Pyza who sang "Old MacDonald" and ran around the table. Mother looked tired, but said that she had to return to work in her dress salon. After she left, Father put Pyza to bed.

I went to my room and sat at the desk, stonily staring at my homework. But all I could see before my eyes was what had happened in the street.

After a long while, I cooled off somewhat. I felt hurt that Father didn't trust me. Why had he found it necessary to make fools of both of us with his old-fashioned ways in front of a Canadian boy.

There was a knock at the door.

"Come in."

It was Father. He sat down heavily in the chair and asked if I would go with him to a textile factory tomorrow, to pick up some work.

"It's amazing that I have to make a living from my hobbies," he said. "In Poland I used to love painting, particularly flowers. I showed a friend of mine several of the jewellery boxes I had painted in Poland. He liked them a lot and told me that there is an opening for a part-time screen printer in the textile factory where he works. I am to pick up some designs for their floral patterns and work on them at home."

Father grew silent.

My heart softened. How he struggles to make a living, I thought. For a moment I forgot all the hurt. Enthusiastically I agreed to go with him.

When Monday came around I worried about how I would explain Father's outburst to Paul. I needn't have worried. He said only a stiff hello when passing me in the hallway. I hoped that he would stop and chat. I hoped that he might get my telephone number from Miriam, that he was secretly pining away for me. None of that happened.

Over a Coke after school, Miriam told me not to waste my time on Paul.

"If he were a real man, he would have stood behind you, Polachka. He is just a worthless slob."

I had to agree with her.

I went home to turn this event into a story. My folder, which I kept in the old brown suitcase, was now full of little stories, some written during the war, others from the time of the Ghetto and afterwards. The earlier ones were in Polish, of course, but as I learned more English I found that writing in English offered me a challenge. Besides, my written Polish was getting rusty.

The many mistakes that I still made in my English stories

bothered me. After thinking about it for a long time, I decided to send the Ghetto stories to Joshua for correction. Also, I felt that he would be interested in them.

I waited impatiently for an answer but much time went by and no answer came. I was becoming disillusioned even with Joshua. I could not believe that he was the kind of "slob" that Miriam thought Paul to be.

One day I decided to send Joshua a short dry note. After all, I felt that my stories were my very soul and that it was in his possession.

> *Dear Joshua,*
>
> *It's been a long time since I've heard from you. You must be busy with either basketball or other important matters that occupy a serious student. As for me, I am doing fine. Life here has become rather . . . But after all, studying has some merit. I really don't need too many people confusing my life. It's a bother.*
>
> *Well, I hope you're well and happy,*
> *Elizabeth*
>
> *P.S. If you are through with my stories could you please return them? Thanks.*

After I mailed the note, I felt better. He deserved it, I thought.

Schoolwork was still tedious, and my soul was filled with bitterness. Nevertheless, I continued to write stories in my uncertain English, using a Polish word here and there. Writing was like entering a world of words — where I felt almost totally free.

One day a letter from Joshua arrived. I tore open the envelope.

Dearest Lizzie,

Your note was like a bucket of ice poured over my head. I could not understand such coldness coming from you. First of all, I didn't write to you for sometime because my mother was very ill with flu, so ill that she was put in hospital and I had to help run the household. Then I caught the flu and was sick for several weeks.

Your letter made me feel so unhappy that I couldn't get either it or you out of my mind. I was then reminded of your stories from the Ghetto, which I regret to say I had not read till a few days ago.

Liz, the stories are unbelievable. I had to show them to my parents (I hope you don't mind). They reacted strangely, I reacted strangely. I mean we felt that some of it sounded almost unreal. We have read in the newspapers what happened to the Jews in Europe, yet you were actually there and experienced it. Hardly anyone in Rockville ever talks about it. Most people behave as if it never happened. The other day in school I tried to say something about it to one of my basketball team pals, who is Gentile. He just looked at me blankly and said, "Let's play ball." For us here, having lived peacefully and growing up as ordinary Canadians, these stories are difficult to fathom. In fact, this whole issue seems to be surrounded by secrecy and silence.

Maybe I understand you better now and why your letter was so lacking in trust. Don't you have any faith, Liz, in the goodness of people, in God, in the possibility that someone could care? Are you still filled with hate?

I am returning your stories, as you asked. You will notice that I have taken some liberties in correcting your English, which I find has improved.

Please write soon,

Love,

Joshua

P.S. I am sending you a small gift.

Something shiny fell out of the envelope. I picked up the tiny object with uncertain fingers and examined it. It was a star, the kind worn on the arms of Jewish people in the Warsaw Ghetto, the Star of David. Attached to it was a thin gold chain. I put it around my neck and re-read the letter.

Joshua was right. Maybe I was mistrustful and bitter and full of hate still. There was such secrecy and silence surrounding the murder of our people that even my parents and their friends hardly ever mentioned it. It was as if they were ashamed to talk about it.

I wrote back to Joshua immediately, saying that I was sorry about his and his mother's flu, and that I hoped everyone was better. Most of all, I apologized for the coldness of my letter. Although I knew that I cared for Joshua, somehow I couldn't sign the letter "Love, Liz."

After thinking hard about it, I figured out why it was so difficult to write something that most Canadian teenagers wouldn't think twice about.

In Polish, the word love has a much stronger meaning. You wouldn't say "I love oranges" in Polish; you would say "I like oranges." In English you can use the word "love" for just about anything. It's used loosely, I thought, and therefore loses some of its true meaning. I wasn't really sure what Joshua meant when he wrote, "Love, Joshua."

I asked Miriam about the "love" business. She told me that I was too analytical and paranoid. "Joshua sounds like the kind of a guy who means what he says," she told me.

June brought summer and the end of school. My report card showed good marks in Latin and French, a mere pass in English and a C- in history and geography. I failed biology and math. Mother came to school with me to see the principal in hopes of convincing him not to make me repeat grade nine. They worked out a compromise.

Because I was good in languages, I could study grade ten French and Latin with a tutor during the summer and write grade ten exams in August. With these subjects out of the way, I would concentrate on the other subjects, do the same thing next summer, and maybe skip a year if I showed great improvement.

"You were putting in too many hours at the deli and in your social life," said Mother on the way home. "There is no room in your life now for frivolities. They will have to stop."

They did.

On sweltering summer days, when other kids were playing tennis, swimming and going to the country, I studied Latin and French. Mother put in extra hours at the salon to help with expenses, and had to arrange baby sitting for Pyza at someone's home.

Father still worked at home on the floral designs, but his health was failing. He could only stand up at his work table for short periods of time. I missed Miriam, who had gone to the country with her parents. The brightest moments were Joshua's letters, which I would pick up at Miriam's mailbox with the key she gave me. It was a thrill to hear that he would come to Montreal at Chanukah with his basketball team. But that was still such a long way off.

The Montreal heat made study difficult. On especially hot days I would sit on the balcony unable to concentrate on the work in front of me. Instead, I contemplated dramatic things. Should I jump into the river, or slash my wrists like a heroine in a movie?

One night I dreamed about being pursued by men on horses, high up in the Caucasus Mountains. I was the Princess Dzavaha, falling into the River Kura and being rescued by a beautiful boy who resembled Joshua . . . but he disappeared and I continued to fall deeper and deeper into the water . . .

I woke up with a start.

"You had a bad dream, little one," said my father's voice. I breathed easier. He took me in his arms and held me. It felt safe. But I realized how pitifully thin he had become. I hugged him as his voice continued softly in the dark.

"Don't worry so much about school," he said. When your English improves you will do better. It will be a struggle. But you must promise me, that no matter what, you will pursue your education. Because without it you will never get anywhere. Do you promise?"

"I promise, Papa," I said fervently, and felt less anxious. Father had always been able to make me feel better when I was low. Just as he was about to leave, he noticed the star dangling on my neck.

"What's this?" he asked. I told him that it was a gift from Joshua. He thought for a moment, then said, "It's an especially thoughtful gift. I remember him. He is a very fine boy, Slavenka."

It felt like old times when Father and I were so close. I slept soundly for the rest of the night.

In August I wrote my Latin and French exams and passed both with an A. My parents rejoiced.

My sixteenth birthday was a happy occasion, which Miriam and Mother organized at our home. Father was in good spirits. He gave me a carved jewellery box on which he had painted a large, bright sunflower. I kept Joshua's star in it when I took it off at night.

My joy was short-lived. The next week at a medical check-up, the doctor said that Father would need another operation.

A few weeks later, the day after the operation, Mother came home from the hospital with a sorrowful face.

"It's cancer," she said. Her voice was unusually deep. "Papa doesn't know. He thinks he will get better, but the doctors are not at all hopeful. They didn't diagnose it soon enough, and now it has spread into his stomach and liver."

I felt numb. I didn't want to believe it. Father must get better. He must. After all, we had survived the war and immigration. Why should this happen now?

But Father didn't get better.

During this time, Miriam often took me away to a movie, or to her house. I was glad to get away from home. But in the end there was no avoiding it. I'd return home in the dark. No one waited for me or asked where I had been. My sister was asleep and Mother was at work. Father lay in his bed moaning in pain. I heard him say, "I wish I were dead, I wish I were dead," over and over again. There was nothing I could do, save making him tea and talking with him for a bit when the pain lessened.

The smell of sickness was beginning to pervade the house like the smell of old blood. I sat in the living room listening to Father toss and moan. I was angry, so angry. Couldn't the doctors do something? I thought. Must this suffering go on and on and on?

One morning I woke up to a commotion in the apartment. It was the ambulance people. They came and took Father to the hospital. Mother went with him. I stared at his rumpled bed, and in spite of a terrible emptiness in my heart, I felt relieved. His suffering had become too hard to bear.

It was midnight when Mother came home. The apartment was cold and dark. She drifted into my room like a shadow, and said in a hushed voice, "Papa is no longer with us."

CHAPTER 15

Joshua
(MONTREAL, 1949)

IT TOOK ME A long time to get over Father's death.

Eventually, however, the pain lessened. During this period, my faithful Miriam helped me. Her house became a second home to me.

She helped me take my mind off my father's death with her chatter. We never ran out of things to talk about, especially boys. She had finally settled on Mark as her steady, and they often invited me out for a movie and a soda afterwards.

After so much bad luck, life was becoming easier for us at home. Mother's dressmaking became so successful that she and her partner opened an elegant shop on Sherbrooke Street. Our money worries finally behind us, Mother was able to hire a Russian immigrant woman to help with the house and take care of Pyza. So Pyza wouldn't feel too lonely with Father gone and Mother at the shop, I always put aside some time to spend alone with her.

The best thing was Joshua's visit at Chanukah. His uncle had moved to Montreal from the prairies, so now Joshua had a place to stay and a reason to visit more often.

I couldn't believe how he had changed. Now seventeen, he had grown taller and was even more handsome than when I had met him in Rockville. Having skipped a grade, he was now in grade eleven. Once Miriam met him, she assured me that he was a great "catch."

It was miraculous seeing him at our dining room table, lighting the Chanukah candles in the menorah he had given me the year before. I looked at him through the flaming candles and felt an overwhelming love for him. But I wasn't certain if his feelings were the same. Perhaps he just cared for me as one would for a friend.

Mother said that I was too young to feel this way. But Miriam said that I was long overdue. She told me that she started having those feelings when she was twelve!

A few days later, Joshua was invited to come with us to the Rosenbergs for dinner. Dressed to kill as always, Ina ignored me and put on a show for Joshua. It seemed to me — or was I just imagining it? — that he wasn't altogether indifferent to her, and kept on looking at her tight black sweater. He certainly paid her a lot of attention.

I was wearing a boring loose white blouse Mother had

made me put on, a pleated navy skirt and low-heeled shoes. I felt as though I was being swept along by waves of unfamiliar feelings, both pleasant and painful. Later on, Miriam told me that I was jealous, and had good reason to be.

When Joshua left again for Rockville, I felt confused and lonely. He never said anything about Ina, and I was too embarrassed to ask.

In the months that followed, I worked really hard at school, trying to keep my promise to Father. Even though I was making progress, I often felt ridiculous, being the oldest girl in my grade nine class.

Sometimes when I was alone at home, with Pyza in bed and Mother out working, it seemed as if I could still hear sounds of Father tossing about. I struggled with my grief as one would struggle with an enemy. I cried and had bad dreams. I wrote to Joshua about it and anxiously awaited an answer.

In the meantime, Miriam decided that I needed a break, and took me shopping for clothes, so I wouldn't look so dowdy the next time Joshua came to Montreal.

"Clothes for girls our age are boring," said Miriam browsing through the teen girls' wear at Morgan's. "I mean they're so juvenile. There is no difference between what thirteen-year-olds and sixteen-year-olds wear, unless you spend gobs of money and shop at boutiques." She looked at me with a roguish smile and added, "Like your friend Ina, for example."

Then I saw it: hanging next to a fitting room was the outfit, the one I'd been looking for all my life! A dark orange skirt with black tassels at the bottom, and a matching triangular scarf.

"Not bad," judged Miriam. "But your mother will have a fit. It's so flashy."

"Well, I'm in a flashy mood," I said. After a while, my enthusiasm diminished at the thought of what Mother would say when she saw the outfit.

"If you like it, buy it," said Miriam with her usual optimism, "but at least get a snug black sweater to go with it."

On that one shopping trip we spent all the earnings I had made working at the deli in the past year. We even bought my first pair of high-heeled shoes in black leather.

On the way home I stopped at the mail box and, to my absolute joy, found a letter from Joshua.

Dearest Liz,

I do understand what you are suffering. I know that you still find the world a hostile place, and your father has always been someone who had protected you in it. It is sad for you to think of yourself as "alone in the hostile world." But you make one mistake. You are not alone. I know that your mother is busy, but I am certain that you could talk to her. After all, she, too, shares the pain of your loss. Then you have Miriam who truly loves you. And what about me, Liz? Am I not someone who cares about you, even if I am in another town?

By the way, I am coming to Montreal again at the end

of March, when the school has an Easter break. We are
playing Westmount High, and I'll be staying at my
uncle's. We'll have a great time. I've written to Mark,
and he and Miriam are going to have a party after the
game. Can I count on you as my date?
Take care now, and no more tragic thoughts.
Lots of love,
Joshua

I read and re-read the letter, savouring each word. There was
so much in it to think about. I read it to Miriam over the
phone.

"Don't read too much into it, Polachka," advised my
friend. "It says what it means. I think it's great that you have
a date. I mean, it's about time. So are you going to wear
your new dress?"

"I guess so," I replied. "Mother hasn't seen it though. So
far it's sitting under my bed. I think I'll go try it on again."

I pulled out the the outfit from under my bed and put it
on with the high-heels. Then I went into Mother's room
and surveyed my image in the mirror. I could hardly recognize myself. I was two inches taller. The skirt was full and
the tassels just swished above the ankles. The black sweater
made me look at least five years older, and when I threw the
scarf over all this, I thought I looked very dramatic. Almost
like a film star. I practised walking and fell over a chair.
Some movie star!

"What's going on here?" called Mother's voice from the doorway.

Oh. Oh!

"Now that looks vulgar!" exclaimed Mother.

"But Mama, all my clothes are so juvenile," I whined. "And Joshua has asked me out to a big party when he comes to Montreal next month," I added, knowing that Mother approved of Joshua.

"Well, you're not exactly an old woman yet. Besides, don't you want to look elegant?" asked Mother. "A boy like Joshua doesn't want to be seen with a sleazy-looking girl. You should return it to the store, and I'll see if I can pick you up a more suitable dress."

Feeling like a naughty child, I took off the outfit and placed it in its box under the bed. I did not intend to take it back. Instead, I called Miriam and consulted with her, half-whispering on the phone.

First she had to tell me "I told you so," and then she offered to keep the outfit for me in her room so that I could change into it at her house on the day of the party. After hanging up, I surveyed the piles of homework on my desk. Why couldn't March be tomorrow instead of two months from now?

I sat down to work on math and struggled with it for an hour. Then I turned to something more satisfying. In English class, Miss Bird had asked us to write an essay based on something we knew well, about a person, a place or an event. The best essay in grade nine and ten would win a prize. I knew that I didn't have much of a chance because of my weak grammar and awkward sentence structure, but Miss Bird once said that I had a knack for good description.

I leafed through the stories I had written. Among the pieces written half in English and half in Polish was one entitled "The Gardener of Children." It needed a lot of work, but I thought it would make a good essay.

The story was about Dr. Janusz Korczak and his orphanage — the one I had visited in the Ghetto, having seen him tending his flowers on his balcony. From then on I had the image of him tending orphans with the same loving care that he gave his flowers.

I reworked the story, trying to maintain the images of gardener and garden, but I knew there must be a lot of mistakes in the grammar. At first this discouraged me. Then I had an idea. Since I owed Joshua a letter, I scribbled a note asking him to read and correct the English in my story. Then I ran to the post office with the envelope and mailed it right away.

February flew by in a hazy maze of history, geography and math. I had little time for socializing, save for once a week when Miriam and I would see a movie.

One bit of rainbow was a short letter from Joshua.

Dear Liz,

I am returning your story. It was very moving and I liked it very much. I doubt that very many Canadians have heard of Dr. Korczak. Your metaphor of the gar-

dener is truly poetic and fitting. Your English is much better than you think. Of course there were mistakes. But with a few corrections here and there, I think you have a good essay. Please let me know soon what happens.

Love,

Joshua

I looked at the essay with its corrections and studied them. Then I set out to copy it and when I had finished, I re-read it.

THE GARDENER OF CHILDREN
by Elizabeth Lenski, grade 9

There once was a man who loved children. He cultivated them as a gardener would cultivate flowers.

He believed that children need plenty of greenery, fresh air, sunshine and love to grow up happy and healthy in both body and spirit. Violence had no place in his garden, and no flower was inferior to another.

He was a doctor of medicine, a pediatrician, and an author of children's books. Although born a Jew with the name of Henryk Goldszmidt, he was better known by his pen name of Janusz Korczak.

Throughout his life Dr. Korczak tried to bridge the differences between the Jews and the Christians of Poland. Before the Second World War, he ran one home for the Polish orphans and another for the Jewish ones.

During the Second World War, in the Warsaw Ghetto, where hundreds of thousands of Jewish people were incarcerated by the Nazis, the Doctor ran a home for Jewish orphans. Each day, hundreds died of starvation and disease while the trains to the death camps carried off thousands of Jews to die.

Like a gardener whose flowers were being choked by the evil weeds of violence and disease, Dr. Korczak and his assistants tended the sick, the sad and the lonely children of the Ghetto. He was their doctor, teacher and parent.

The orphanage was a miniature society unto itself, based on Dr. Korczak's beliefs that children have rights and should be offered choices. They need to earn self-respect by carrying out tasks that contribute to the welfare of others and be rewarded. At the heart of this society was the Children's Court, whose code of honour encouraged forgiveness, honesty, charity and defence of the weak. The court was headed by five judges, and met every Saturday. It listened to all complaints and decided on all punishment. With the exception of one adult who was present to take minutes, children held all the positions in the court.

Although strength and health were waning in his aging body, although food, clothing and medical supplies were scarce in the Ghetto, Dr. Korczak was relentless in his efforts. He begged and borrowed to provide his children with essentials. He also tried to bring some joy and a sense of belonging into the orphanage.

There were celebrations of Jewish holidays such as Passover and Rosh Hashanah, the Jewish New Year. The children would put on a concert or a play and invite visitors. The study of Hebrew was encouraged, among other subjects of interest to the children.

The children helped with the daily chores, studied, played and even laughed, a rare sight in those tragic days. Upon leaving, the visitors could look up to the balcony of the orphanage. If it were summer, they could see the elderly, white-bearded Doctor watering flowers with the same care that he bestowed upon the children. He continued his work to the very end.

On the sixth of August 1942, German soldiers came and ordered the orphans, the assistants and Dr. Korczak to line up outside the orphanage and march to *Umschlagplatz* deportation depot. Although they did not know it, their destination was to be a death camp.

Dr. Korczak walked through the Ghetto streets at the head of two hundred children, carrying one small child and holding another by the hand. Witnesses said it was the most orderly, dignified and tragic march ever seen in the Ghetto.

At the station, they were loaded into the crowded cattle cars that reeked of disinfectants, and were sent to Treblinka Concentration Camp. None returned or were ever heard of again. It was rumoured that Dr. Korczak was given the opportunity of freeing himself but declined to leave his children. We may never know the truth, but the legend of Dr. Korczak lives on: how he planted stars in the souls of children who were forced to live in the Garden of Darkness.

I handed in the essay to Miss Bird without any great hopes of winning. The results were to be announced in May.

One day, Mother came home from her salon with a parcel. "Here is your reward for working so hard," she said, handing me the parcel. I opened it and found a plain navy-blue dress made of heavy cotton. It was long and had a full skirt, short sleeves and a collar. I didn't think much of it. It was too "elegant" and didn't have the flash of my orange one.

"Thanks, Mama, it's lovely," I lied, and kissed her, not wanting to appear ungrateful.

The date of Joshua's visit was approaching. Miriam and Mark talked non-stop about the party they were having afterwards. I was becoming nervous. This visit was going to be different because it was the first time Joshua had asked me for a date. It meant something more than just being old friends.

One day Miriam phoned and told me something that made me feel ill. She and Mark had gone to a party thrown by one of Mark's friends. The friend's date at the party was Ina Rosenberg.

"You're kidding," I said half in tears. "Does that mean that she is coming to our party for the Rockville team?"

"She might," replied Miriam. "She certainly behaves the way you've described. She climbs all over Tom, and makes goo-goo eyes at all the other fellows. But when she speaks to a girl, she is as snooty as they come. And the way she dresses!" Miriam's voice seemed to be equal parts envy and outrage. "She was wearing a bright red silk dress with a plunging neckline that must have cost a pretty penny. Your orange outfit would wither and die next to it."

I couldn't sleep all night. I kept imagining horrible things. Ina the snake, Ina the vampire. During the day I couldn't concentrate on school work. I was afraid that I would lose Joshua to Ina.

Easter exams were trials of unspeakable hardship. I studied till morning, cramming, reading over my notes in the washroom just before the tests. Then, with the exams finally over, I had nothing to do but wait till after the Easter break for results. I started working for Mr. Yankelman at the deli again, but Joshua's visit occupied my thoughts constantly. I spent a lot of time with Miriam, who liked Mother's dress better than the one I had picked.

"It has more class, even if it isn't sexy," she said.

"I don't know whether I want to be boringly classy or just look sexy," I replied. But secretly, I wanted to outdo Ina.

We decided that I would start out in Mother's dress, and if I absolutely didn't like myself in it, I would change to the orange. Miriam was going to wear a slinky royal-blue dress, which went well with her red hair. I felt so mousy. What could I do to be different, and to make Joshua really admire me?

The day of Joshua's visit arrived. The game was scheduled for Sunday afternoon, and afterwards there was the party. I asked for Sunday off from the deli, but Mr. Yankelman came down with the flu, and there was no one to take over since Miriam still worked only on weekday afternoons. I was so disappointed but there was nothing I could do.

When we talked about it on the phone, Joshua said he would pick me up at the deli after the game.

Never was the work at the deli as irksome as that Sunday. It seemed as if the whole Jewish Quarter came in for salami. People wanted sandwiches and placed orders for Passover. They pushed and shouted. I felt like just hanging up my apron and leaving them, but when I looked at the impatient grimaces that distorted their faces, I laughed to myself. That got me through the crisis.

When five minutes to six arrived, the deli was still full. I was a mess. How could I go to a party smelling of herring and smoked meat? At six o'clock sharp I went to close the door.

"The deli is now closed," I said firmly to a couple of disappointed people at the door and went back to serve the remaining customers. After they left, I tidied up quickly, not really doing a very good job. Then I ran to the washroom to get myself ready before Joshua came. In fact he was fifteen minutes late and that helped. I turned off the lights, locked the door, and waited impatiently outside in the doorway of the deli. It was dark and chilly.

Six thirty arrived and still no Joshua. Again I started imagining all sorts of things. Ina snaking up to Joshua and charming him into forgetting all about me. Joshua must have got hurt during the game! What else could have happened? I was tired of waiting and started to leave for home, when Joshua suddenly appeared around the corner.

He was all smiles, his eyes were bright. He wore grey pants, a white shirt with a navy tie and a maroon sweater. His open jacket had a crest that said "The Rockville Lions." He looked terrific.

"We won, we won!" he said excitedly, giving me a hug. "That's why I am late. They wouldn't let me leave." He paused and looked at me closely. "Is something wrong?"

"Oh nothing," I said. "Just a hard day at the deli." I felt deflated, even though I was happy that Joshua's team had won.

We walked to my place, catching up on the latest news. At home Joshua talked with Mother and played with Pyza, while I dressed. I put on the dress Mother gave me, with my new black shoes and the gold earrings I borrowed from Miriam. I looked at myself in the mirror and felt neither pretty nor ugly. I dabbed some mascara on and lipstick. My hair wouldn't stay in place. I decided to make the best of things, though I couldn't help feeling nervous. At the back of my mind lurked the possibility that Ina might show up at the party.

"You look lovely," said Joshua. "I've never seen you really dressed up before."

We took a streetcar to the party at Miriam's house. It took us only fifteen minutes to get there; all the while we talked about old times at Rockville.

It wasn't until we walked into the house filled with people that it really struck me. This was our first official date.

When they saw Joshua, everyone shouted and raised their glasses of Coke.

"Twenty baskets!" someone yelled.

"A genius," shouted another.

Joshua was immediately surrounded by a group of fellows. Not really knowing what to do with myself, I started helping Miriam with the food.

"You look swell, Polachka. Are you going to change into your orange dress?" asked Miriam.

"I don't know. Wouldn't Joshua think it silly?"

Miriam shrugged her shoulders. "Do what pleases you, but if I were you I'd stay the way you are."

I decided to take Miriam's advice, wondering if I might have felt more sparkly in the orange dress.

"Do you think Ina might show up?" I asked Miriam.

"So what if she does. You look better. And anyhow, Joshua is not about to go after Ina," said Miriam in a decisive tone of voice.

I began to feel better about things. It was exciting to be with someone as popular as Joshua. I was proud of him, even if he was busy talking to the guys and seemed to have forgotten that I existed.

The place was becoming more crowded. People were coming and going. The music blared. Miriam said that I should go and stand with Joshua since I was his date. Awkwardly, I made my way through the crowd.

"Where have you been?" asked Joshua when I walked up. He put his arm around me and enthusiastically introduced me to his friends. I'd had no idea he had noticed that I wasn't there. I felt warm all over, standing next to him, and became aware of the girls' admiring glances cast in our direction.

More people came in the door. There was a commotion, and laughter, and Ina walked into the room as if she owned it. Everyone turned to look at her.

She was wearing a tight black strapless dress, and a white stole carelessly thrown over one shoulder. Her black hair was held up with rhinestone combs, and long rhinestone earrings dangled from her ears. She looked sensational.

When she saw me next to Joshua her eyes narrowed like a snake's. I looked quickly at him. Like those of every other boy in the room, his eyes were drawn to Ina.

She glided across the room and looked down at me, her spiky red heels giving her the extra height. "Oh," she said haughtily, "it's you."

Then she pointedly turned away from me towards Joshua. The tone of her voice changed to sugary. "Joshua, I saw the game. You're a real hero. Isn't he, everyone?"

A cheer swept the room. Now that she had won them over, she hooked her arm through Joshua's.

"Can we get me something to eat?" she asked in the same sweet tone of voice. "I am simply famished."

Joshua appeared stunned as she led him away into the dining room. People obligingly moved aside to make room for them.

Through a fog, I saw Miriam's shocked face staring at me

with concern. I wanted to die. Like a curled-up autumn leaf, I drifted towards the front door, opened it, and ran out into the street.

It was dark and windy. I ran, my mind full of all the other times I had run away: from the lineup in the Ghetto; from the sirens and the thunder of bombs; from the taunting of the kids in Rockville; and now from Ina and Joshua.

I stumbled and fell next to a bench in a park. I picked myself up, holding onto the iron railing of the bench, and sat down. My palms and knees smarted from scratches, and the hem of my dress was torn. It started to rain. I shivered in the cold. I was ruined, I thought. My life might as well have come to an end.

Suddenly I heard running footsteps and someone dropped next to me onto the bench. It was Joshua. He was out of breath. Automatically, I moved away, wanting no part of him now. Silence engulfed us as the wind whined through the trees. Rain fell on our faces. He made a move to wipe a raindrop off my cheek. I flinched.

"Get away from me," I choked out. "Just go away and leave me alone."

"Liz, stop all this," he said, taking hold of my shoulders and turning me to face him. "I know why you're mad. I couldn't help what happened; she took me by surprise. I shouldn't have let her embarrass you. But by the time I figured out what she was up to, you had left. Miriam told me which direction you'd gone, so I ran after you."

I still couldn't bring myself to look at him, so he gently placed his hand against my cheek and turned my face to meet his eyes.

"Liz, I don't want someone like Ina. I despise the way she dresses and flaunts herself. It's you I love, Lizzie. I love the way you talk and the way you dress — everything. You didn't have to run from her. You don't have to run from anyone or anything. When will you feel that you have the same rights as everyone else in this world?"

Had I really heard him say that he loved me? I was still stiff when he moved closer. Slowly, he put his arms around me and I let him kiss me. We kissed for a long time, my tears and the rain all mixed into one.

"I love you too, Joshua," I said, still uncertain. Could he really mean it? All these emotions still scared me. Yet I knew I had loved Joshua ever since we were together at Chanukah.

"In a year's time I will be at school here in Montreal. Will you wait for me?" he asked. I nodded, unsure of my voice. He smiled and pulled his signet ring off his finger and slipped it onto mine.

As he walked me home with his arm around me, all I could see was Joshua's gold ring shining on my finger.

Miriam telephoned when I got home, and I told her about our talk in the park and the ring.

"I am so happy for you, Polachka," replied Miriam quietly, with much feeling. Then she added, "You should have seen the look on Ina's face when Joshua left her to run after you."

The next day Joshua told me that Eva Schmidt was in town for a girl's basketball game. The YMCA was having a get-together of all the basketball players from the four teams, and he asked me to come with him. At first I said no. But then I remembered what he had said in the park about not having to run away, and decided to go.

When we reached the YMCA, I saw Eva talking to several of the girls from Rockville. Some of them had been in the group that chased me to my hiding place.

Joshua guided me into the crowd, and Eva saw me as we approached. She faced me from where she was standing and inched her way over.

"Hi, Elizabeth," she said. "I am sorry about your father. Joshua told me about him."

She seemed friendly enough. I remembered what Joshua had said about Eva having suffered during the war as a German-Canadian. It must have been difficult to be singled out as an enemy. I didn't think we could ever be good friends, but I felt secure enough to bury past resentments. Still, I had doubts. Eva's being nice to me didn't mean that she had changed her opinion about the Jews.

I smiled at her and said, "Thanks and congratulations on making the basketball team. I remember how hard you worked for it."

She smiled back. We chatted for a short while, then said goodbye.

"Do come and visit us," she said, and sounded as though she meant it. We parted on friendly terms.

The week went by as in a fairy tale. Joshua and I saw each other every day. And then the week was over and Joshua left.

CHAPTER 16

The Old Brown Suitcase

(MONTREAL, 1949)

SCHOOL STARTED AGAIN.

When the exam results came in, I found that I had merely passed the subjects I had previously failed. That was encouraging, but I knew I'd have to get at least a B if I wanted to skip a grade and get back to the same class as Miriam. I'll do it somehow, I promised myself.

In English class Miss Bird said she would announce the winner of the prize for the best composition at awards night. I felt pretty pessimistic, despite what Joshua had said about my story.

The awards night took place in the school auditorium where all the parents and relatives had gathered. Both

Mother and Pyza were there as well.

Miss Bird began by saying that everyone had written a good story. "I am really proud of all the grade nine and ten students," she said. "Choosing the winner was a most difficult task. There is, however, one story that stands out for its human content, on a subject that touches all our hearts, and that subject is the fate of innocent children. The first prize, I am happy to announce, goes to a girl who has lived through the war in Poland."

Heat rushed to my head, and I began to tremble. It must be me. Who else here has been in the war? I looked around the room. No one. I knew that.

"The story is called 'The Gardener of Children,' written by Elizabeth Lenski in grade nine," said Miss Bird. "Elizabeth, please come up on the stage and claim your prize." Everyone clapped. Somehow I made my way up the stairs onto the stage. Miss Bird handed me a book tied with a red ribbon. It was a copy of *Anne of Green Gables*. I was so overcome with emotion that I almost thanked everyone in Polish. For a moment I remembered myself in my sunflower costume back in Warsaw, on the stage — a little girl dancing with her back to the audience. But this time I wasn't going to do things backwards. I corrected myself in time and managed to say a few words of gratitude — in English. Everyone clapped again, and I walked off the stage.

I was overcome with happiness. If only Father had been here to see me.

The day after the awards was Pyza's fourth birthday. We

had a party with a cake that Miriam baked. Pyza had just blown out her candles when the phone rang.

I ran to answer it and heard the familiar, "Hi Liz!"

"Hi, Joshua!" I answered, happy to hear his voice. "I won the composition contest!"

"I knew you would," replied Joshua, as if he had never had the slightest doubt. "Congratulations!"

We talked for a few moments longer, making plans for our next meeting.

"I miss you, Joshua," I said at the end of our conversation, no longer afraid to show my feelings.

"I miss you too, Liz," he replied.

After I hung up I went slowly back to the birthday party. Everyone was chatting and eating, but Pyza was nowhere to be seen. I went to look for her and found her in my room. There she was sitting inside my old brown suitcase, tangled in the netting of my sunflower costume.

"Play dress up with Pyza?" she asked, her little chubby hands trying to put on the hat. I dressed her up, pinning the costume with safety pins as it was a bit too big.

"Guess what, little one?" I said. "When Halloween comes, you can wear it, to go trick-or-treating. O.K.?"

Pyza squealed with delight and ran out of the room to show her costume to the guests.

The only things left in the suitcase now were my blond braids, the folder with the stories and two books.

I placed the Polish version of *Anne of Green Gables* on the shelf alongside the Canadian one I had won. Next to it I put the *Princess Dzavaha*, vowing that one day I would translate it into English. Finally, I took my own stories from the suitcase and placed them on my desk. Tomorrow, I said to myself, I'll look through them again, and think about rewriting them.

Now there were only the braids left in the suitcase. As I looked at them I could hear my father's words on that night long ago in Poland when he gave me the suitcase: "You're getting to be a big girl, Slava. Who knows where this suitcase might take you someday."

I locked the suitcase, and went back to the party.

Historical Notes

THE OLD BROWN SUITCASE tells the story of a young refugee named Slava whose experiences occur before, during and after the Second World War. The story crosses the Atlantic Ocean from Europe to North America.

Although her story begins some seventy years ago, it remains relevant today. Wars still continue to occur in many countries, and many governments still do appalling things to individuals and minority groups. Such horrors continue to cause people to leave their native lands and become refugees.

There may be a number of Slavas in your school or neighbourhood. They may have a different name, a different hair colour, a different language or country of origin than the girl in this book. Like Slava, however, they want to fit in, find friends, do well in school, and somehow overcome the weight of their painful past.

In order to understand these new arrivals, it helps to understand where they came from and the events that made them flee. If Slava's story has moved or interested you, remember that each refugee has his or her own story that could fill its own book.

THE HISTORY BEHIND THIS BOOK

The Old Brown Suitcase is a documentary fiction. Although several characters were invented and minor facts and names of places were altered slightly, the story is based on historical events that form the core of the author's own experience. The following notes may clarify some parts of the story.

POLAND lies between Russia on its east side and Germany on its west. It was an independent republic when Germany invaded on September 1, 1939. The Polish army, ill-equipped to fight the efficient war machine of the Third Reich, fell apart after a few weeks of brave resistance. In 1945, at the end of the war, Poland was liberated by the Soviet Army.

WARSAW is the capital of Poland. Before the Second World War it was a beautiful city bustling with commerce, culture and night life. At the war's end in Europe, in January 1945, Warsaw lay in total ruin. Its destruction was staged in three acts. During the German invasion, continuous bombing and shelling destroyed many buildings. In 1943, a large section of the city known as the Warsaw Ghetto was annihilated. Finally, after the Poles staged an uprising in August 1944, Hitler ordered Warsaw to be "levelled to the ground." After looting everything of value, the Nazis divided the city into sections and systematically proceeded to destroy it. While this was happening, the Soviet Army remained on the other side of the Vistula River, cynically waiting until the uprising was crushed. The destruction included the burning of museums, theatres and archives that held irreplaceable documents and treasures of Polish culture. After the war ended, the people of Poland set about rebuilding their beloved city.

THE JEWS OF POLAND were a thriving community before the war. In the 1930s there were over two and a half million Jews in Poland, comprising approximately ten percent of the Polish population. Jewish society included both secular and religious Jews who were active participants in the business, the industrial and the professional affairs of Polish life. There were many Jewish citizens such as doctors, lawyers and engineers, who assimilated into Polish society through professional interaction with the Gentiles. Nevertheless, the majority were poor tradespeople and industrial workers who struggled to keep their families fed.

Once the Nazis established themselves in Poland, they began to persecute all Jews. They deprived them of their

homes, businesses and professions. They forced them to do hard labour and menial tasks. They ordered them to wear arm bands with the Star of David. Most often these stars were yellow in colour. In Warsaw, however, they were blue. Jews suffered public humiliation and lynching. Then they were thrown into ghettos and deported to death camps where they were tortured, starved, gassed and burned. At the end of the war in 1945, only 30,000 Jews were left in Poland. These survived only by chance, by running, hiding in barns, villages, basements and attics. Some were fortunate to find kind Christian individuals who offered help with housing and food. The ones in the concentration camps of Poland, miraculously still alive at the end of the war, were rescued by the Russians.

THE WARSAW GHETTO (1939–1943) was sealed off in mid-November 1940. Some four hundred thousand Jews, thirty-seven percent of the Warsaw population, were forced to live in a space of about 3.5 square kilometres, or 4.5 percent of the city's area. This area, decreed by the Nazis to become the Warsaw Ghetto, had been the Jewish quarter of the city before the war, where many Jews enjoyed a vibrant communal Jewish life. As more and more Jewish people were forced in from neighbouring towns and the countryside, the population of the Ghetto increased. Starvation, typhus and Nazi raids accelerated the death rate among the people with unbelievable speed. Then the deportations began, with thousands of Jews being sent to death camps. In April 1943, when the Germans decided to liquidate the Ghetto, a group of young Jewish fighters staged a brave battle against heavily armed German troops. The battle lasted for about a month. Afterwards the Germans sent the remaining handful of Jews to concentration camps, burned the Ghetto, and ordered destroyed whatever was left. The former Jewish quarter became a large field of rubble.

It was in the Warsaw Ghetto where the famous Janusz Korczak and his assistants looked after two hundred orphaned children. He was a pediatrician and a writer of children's stories, who dedicated his life to orphaned children. Before the war, he organized both a Christian and a Jewish orphanage in Warsaw, but was forced to move the Jewish one to the Warsaw Ghetto. One day Janusz Korczak, also known as Henryk J. Goldszmidt, his assistants and the children were forced out of the orphanage and sent to the Treblinka death factory where they were all murdered.

Further Reading

Adler, Stanislaw. *In The Warsaw Ghetto*. Transl. Sara Chmielewska Philip. Jerusalem: Yad-Vashem, 1982.

Frank, Anne. 1947; *The Diary of Young Girl*. The Definitive Edition. New York: Doubleday, 1995.

Gutman, Yisrael. *The Jews of Warsaw, 1939–1943*. Transl. Ina Friedman. Bloomington: Indiana University Press, 1989.

Hersey, John. *The Wall*. New York: Random House, 1988 (original publication in 1950).

Hyams, Joseph. *A Field of Buttercups*. Englewood Cliffs, N.J.: Prentice Hall, 1968.

Kalman, Judith. *The Country of Birches*. Vancouver: Douglas & McIntyre, 1998.

Kahn, Leon. *No Time to Mourn*. Vancouver: Ronsdale Press, 2004.

Korczak, Janusz. *Ghetto Diary*. New York: Holocaust Library, 1978.

Levine, Karen. *Hana's Suitcase*. Toronto: Second Story Press, 2002.

Lifton, Betty Jean. *The King of Children: A Biography of Janusz Korczak*. New York: Farrar, Straus & Giroux, 1988.

Matas, Carol. *Daniel's Story*. New York: Scholastic, 1993.

Schoenberner, Gerhard. *The Yellow Star: The Persecution of the Jews in Europe 1933–1945*. New York: Fordham University Press, 2004.

Watts, Irene. N. *Goodbye Marianne*. Toronto: Tundra Books, 1998.

Wiesel, Elie. *Night*. New York: Farrar, Straus & Giroux, 2005 (original publication in 1960).

FILMS AND/OR VIDEOS

A Day in the Warsaw Ghetto by Jack Kuper, 1991.

Korczak by Andrzej Wajda, English subtitles, 1989.

Memorandum by Donald Brittain (Canadian Film Board), 1965.

My Mother, My Hero by Daniel Leipnik, 2002 (includes Lillian Boraks-Nemetz discussing her experience in the Ghetto).

Schindler's List by Steven Spielberg, 1993.

Uprising by Jon Avnet, 2001.

The Warsaw Ghetto (three documentary films) by Log-In Productions, 2005.

(The "video" section of the Google browser offers various short films on the Warsaw Ghetto).

About the Author

Lillian Boraks-Nemetz was born in Warsaw, Poland, where she survived the Holocaust as a child. She was incarcerated in the Warsaw Ghetto for eighteen months, then hidden in Polish villages for the remainder of the war, under a false identity. After the war, Lillian and her family fled Poland to make their home in Canada. She graduated from St. Margaret's School in Victoria then married, raised two children and returned to the University of British Columbia to complete her Master's Degree in Comparative Literature. Lillian has written poetry and semi-autobiographical fiction, including two sequels to her award-winning novel, *The Old Brown Suitcase*. She lives in Vancouver and teaches Creative Writing at the University of British Columbia's Writing Centre.

Marquis imprimeur inc.

Québec, Canada
2008